Western Fictioneers Presents:

WOLF CREEK:

Bloody Trail

By Ford Fargo

Western Fictioneers

Beneath the mask, **Ford Fargo** *is not one but a posse of America's leading western authors who have pooled their talents to create a series of rip-snortin', old fashioned sagebrush sagas. Saddle up. Read 'em Cowboy! These are the legends of* **Wolf Creek**.

THE WRITERS OF WOLF CREEK, AND THEIR CHARACTERS

Bill Crider - Cora Sloane, schoolmarm

Phil Dunlap - Rattlesnake Jake, bounty hunter

James J. Griffin - Bill Torrance, owner of the livery stable

Jerry Guin - Deputy Marshal Quint Croy

Douglas Hirt - Marcus Sublette, schoolteacher and headmaster

L. J. Martin - Angus "Spike" Sweeney, blacksmith

Matthew Mayo - Rupert "Rupe" Tingley, town drunk

Kerry Newcomb - James Reginald de Courcey, artist with a secret

Cheryl Pierson - Derrick McCain, farmer

Robert J. Randisi - Dave Benteen, gunsmith

James Reasoner - G.W. Satterlee, county sheriff

Frank Roderus - John Nix, barber

Troy D. Smith - Charley Blackfeather, scout; Sam Gardner, town marshal

Clay More - Logan Munro, town doctor

Chuck Tyrell - Billy Below, young cowboy; Sam Jones, gambler

Jackson Lowry - Wilson "Wil" Marsh, photographer

L. J. Washburn - Ira Breedlove, owner of the Wolf's Den Saloon

Matthew Pizzolato - Wesley Quaid, drifter

Appearing as Ford Fargo in this episode:

Clay More (Dr. Logan Munro)- Chapter 1 & 2
James J. Griffin (Bill Torrance)- Chapter 3 & 4
Troy D. Smith (Charley Blackfeather)- Chapter 5 & 6
James Reasoner (G.W. Satterlee)- Chapter 7 & 8
L. J. Martin (Angus "Spike" Sweeney) –Chapter 9 & 10
Cheryl Pierson (Derrick McCain)- Chapter 11 & 12

INTRODUCTION

In Wolf Creek, everyone has a secret.

That includes our author, Ford Fargo—but we have decided to make his identity an *open* secret. Ford Fargo is the "house name" of Western Fictioneers—the only professional writers' organization devoted exclusively to the traditional western, and which includes many of the top names working in the genre today.

Wolf Creek is our playground.

It is a fictional town in 1871 Kansas. Each WF member participating in our project has created his or her own "main character," and each chapter in every volume of our series will be primarily written by a different writer, with their own townsperson serving as the principal point-of-view character for that chapter (or two, sometimes.) It will be sort of like a television series with a large ensemble cast; it will be like one of those Massive Multi-player Role-playing Games you can immerse yourself in online. And it is like nothing that has ever been done in the western genre before.

You can explore our town and its citizens at our website if you wish:

http://wolfcreekkansas.yolasite.com/

Or you can simply turn this page, and step into the dusty streets of Wolf Creek.

Just be careful. It's a nice place to visit, but you wouldn't want to die there.

Troy D. Smith
President, Western Fictioneers
Wolf Creek series editor

CHAPTER ONE

Dr. Logan Munro was conscious of the blood splattered across the front of his shirt. The woman had bled profusely, and although he had moved quickly, he had been unable to protect himself from the gush of the severed vessels.

He looked a mess, but despite himself, he smiled as he walked down the boardwalk on Fourth Street. He was a tall, slim man of almost forty years, with black hair going grey at the temples, and with a pepper and salt mustache. His face was weather-beaten from years spent under the tropical sun of far-off India, and he walked with the upright posture of one who had served in the army, which indeed he had. Dr. Logan Munro had served as a surgeon in three conflicts around the world. First, during the Crimean War, where he had worked at the British Army Hospital in Scutari in Constantinople. There, he'd had the honor of working with the nursing pioneer Florence Nightingale, who had been dubbed the Lady of the Lamp after her habit of making a nightly round of her patients. After a few months, he had been sent to the front with the 21st Regiment of Foot where he had ample opportunity to hone his surgical skills at the Siege of Sevastopol. Then, when the war was over, he had gone to India with the British East India Company

Army, and was unfortunate enough to get embroiled in the Indian Mutiny of 1857. Finally, after settling in America, he had worked his way west and served with the Union in the Civil War.

He had lost his best friend in the first conflict, and he had lost his young wife after the second. Understandably, he had not been in the best of emotional health when he arrived in America. By the time the Civil War ended, he had seen so much killing, had amputated so many mangled limbs and pronounced far too many young folk dead, that he felt more than a part of *him* had died. He had meant to fly as far as possible from civilization, and got as far as the fledgling Kansas town of Wolf Creek— situated in a dogleg-shaped bend of the creek by the same name, a tributary of the Arkansas River. He bought an office there, put up his sign and started doing the only thing he knew how—doctoring. He had intended to bury himself in work, looking after folks from cradle to grave. To his surprise, the town had grown quickly, being the sort of melting pot that people of all creeds and persuasions had gravitated to after the war. Former pro-slavery 'border ruffians' mingled with ardent abolitionist 'Jayhawkers,' but no-one was any the wiser. There was an acceptance that no-one was clean and blameless in war, and if a man wanted to keep his past to himself, that was his business. Then, the Atchison, Topeka and Santa Fe Railroad arrived and caused the town to boom. Cattle drives made for the railhead, and with the influx of cowboys parched from weeks on the trail and with a thirst for copious quantities of drink, an appetite for female company and a desire to gamble their hard-earned money, the fleshpots swelled.

When Logan first put up his shingle and started

seeing patients, the southernmost part of town was South Street. As the town expanded southward, though, another street came into being. It was called Grant Street in honor of the President, but amongst the less deferential cowboys, most of whom hailed from Texas, it was known by the sobriquet of "Useless S. Grant Street." Inevitably, this street marked the boundary between the respectable northern part of the town and the southern, less salubrious part, with its gambling and drinking establishments, its houses of ill repute, and its infamous opium den, owned by an enigmatic Chinese businessman called Tsu Chiao. This newer part of Wolf Creek was known as Dogleg City, being as it nestled into the dogleg of Wolf Creek. And the part that abutted the Creek itself was made up of cribs, hog pens and crude tents where the most haggard of soiled doves plied whatever trade they could. As the town doctor, Logan Munro was often called to minister to them or their clients. At times, he found the downward spiral in some people's lives profoundly depressing.

Yet today was no day to feel sad. A bright sun had risen against a cobalt sky, a fitting harbinger of hope and new life. He straightened his hat, a reflex gesture from his British Army days, and began whistling a refrain from his old regimental song as he swung his bag in jaunty fashion. In his mind, he was whistling along to the pipes of the Scots Fusiliers.

Already, the respectable part of Wolf Creek was starting to come alive, and most of the small business folk had begun their daily toil. He waved to several passers-by and acknowledged the odd rider.

"Ach! You sound annoyingly cheerful for this time of the day, Doctor Munro," barked Frank Kloepfer, the bulky, barrel-chested butcher, as he came out of his doorway. He carried a bucket of sawdust that he was spreading across the floor of his shop. He stroked his luxurious mustache, revealing, in the process, the gap where his two front teeth once resided until they had been knocked out by an irate customer complaining that he had been sold rancid meat. That had been before the big German had dislocated the man's jaw, which it had been Logan's tricky job to reset.

Frank nodded his head at the blood on Logan's shirt. "You had trouble today?"

Logan shook his head with a grin and pointed to the butcher's blood-stained apron. "No trouble, Frank. Just a sign of honest work, the same as yours." He looked down at his shirt and pulled his jacket collar over to try and make the stain less conspicuous.

"But why wouldn't I be cheerful on a day like this?" he asked rhetorically, gazing up at the sky and smiling. "There is nothing like bringing a baby into the world to put a smile on one's face. And that being the case, when you bring two in one go there is twice the reason to be happy."

"Ach, you don't say! That has to be Mrs. Blunkett. She was looking as round as a *kürbis.*" He hesitated as he searched for the word in American, then his eyes widened in delight as it came to him. "As round as a *pumpkin,* when I last saw her." He guffawed and winked lewdly. "Who would think Willie Blunkett was man enough to sire twins!" He rubbed his hands together. "I am guessing they will want steak? Or maybe you want them to ruin some of my good meat and make that heathen British beef tea you go on about."

"Her Majesty, Queen Victoria, sent vast amounts of concentrated beef tea to Florence Nightingale so that she could treat the wounded during the Crimean War. It is a great tonic after illness, and a grand thing for a woman after childbirth," Logan explained enthusiastically. "That, and bosh water from the blacksmith's quenching trough. It's full of iron—just what a woman needs to build new blood. I'll be going over to Spike Sweeney's forge later for a bucket of the stuff so I can make up a bottle or two for her."

He walked on, his mind replaying the birth of the Blunkett twins and the extended episiotomy that he had to cut in order to use the forceps to deliver the head of the second twin, a little boy who had been in a breech, or bottom first, position. The fountain of blood from the spurting vessels severed in his incision had covered him before he had a chance to deflect the spray.

But it was all over now, and Betsy Blunkett and her two babies, one of each sex, were in Martha Pomeroy's capable hands. Martha was an attractive war widow who lived opposite the photographer's studio at the junction of Lincoln and Fifth Street. She happened to be the best midwife he had ever worked with, despite the fact that she had no professional training, and only did it because she found she had a talent at helping woman deliver their babies. It was her personal sadness that her husband had been killed at Baxter Springs, and she had a stillbirth shortly after.

A fine woman, Logan mused for a moment before quickly putting further thought of her from his mind. She and he were both widowed, both vulnerable, but he was not sure whether he could ever allow himself to get involved with another woman. Not after his failure to save Helen, his wife, back in Lucknow.

He crossed Washington Street and tapped on the

window of Ma's Café. The aroma of freshly baked bread, bacon and coffee assailed his nostrils and set his gastric juices flowing.

The said "Ma," matronly Stephanie Adams—another of the many war widows of Wolf Creek—was bustling about serving breakfast to a couple of Joe Nash's boys on one table, and to various Dogleg City revelers who were making their way home or to employment of some sort after a night of debauchery of one form or another. She smiled at him and raised the coffee pot in her hand with a quizzical expression.

"I'll be back," he mouthed through the glass, pointing to the blood stained shirt, then cryptically jerked his thumb over his shoulder.

Ma opened her mouth in mock horror at the sight of the blood. Then, with a laugh, she waved and returned to dispensing coffee to her customers.

Logan laughed and quickened his stride. Although Ma's food was perhaps not as refined as the fare on offer at Isabella's Restaurant on Washington Street, where Antonio Isabella, his wife, and family served out Italian cuisine to the more discerning palates in Wolf Creek, the merry widow knew how to satisfy a man's hunger. Logan tended to spread his patronage among the various eateries, but more often than not, he breakfasted at her establishment. She had an uplifting nature and she never tired of imitating his strange accent that three countries, three wars and a whole lot of living had jumbled into a sort of Scottish patois.

He turned right onto South Street and found his way barred by Marshal Sam Gardner and Fred Garvey, one of his deputies. The marshal was a tall, wiry man in his mid-thirties. His hair hung down to his shoulders, and the goatee he sported was coal black and well-groomed, just like the rest of him. He wore a wide-brimmed hat and frock coat, with a fancy vest, ribbon tie and expensive polished boots. The ivory-handled twin revolvers strapped to his sides implied his usefulness with guns. He had been a U.S. Cavalry officer during the war and had fought with distinction. He was typical of the cavalry types that Logan had seen in the Crimea and in India; brave without doubt, yet with an arrogance and self-belief that could stray into recklessness.

Fred Garvey was a complete contrast. He was a short, stocky man in his middle years with a totally different idea about dress. His clothes were starched clean, and strictly functional, almost like a uniform. But, whereas Gardner was obviously one used to leading and being obeyed, Fred was clearly one who knew his place, and who would happily carry out his superior's orders. His unhurried Georgian drawl was sometimes misconstrued by folk who didn't know him. More than one errant cowpoke had incorrectly assumed that he was slow in the uptake, only to find himself on the end of a tongue-lashing, for he was both intelligent and witty. A stickler for the letter of the law, his short stature belied his ability to deal with anyone who infringed any of the town's statutes.

"Have you been in the wars, Doc?" Fred asked, looking at Logan's bloody clothing with a smile.

"In a manner of speaking. Betsy Blunkett had twins this morning. I'm on my way to Li Wong's Laundry."

Sam Gardner smiled sarcastically. "I thought you didn't cotton to our Chinese friends, Doctor Munro?"

"Then you thought wrong, Marshal," replied Logan, deliberately using the lawman's title, just as he had. "I have no problem with any man, as long as he's honest and doesn't make his living by preying on the weaknesses of others. I believe that the Li family is an absolute asset to Wolf Creek. They are honest and industrious, a good example to many of the residents of the town. I take it you are referring to my views on Tsu Chiao's activities?"

The marshal gave a curt nod.

"Well, there again, I have no personal feelings one way or the other about him as a human being. Who, of any of us, have the right to judge a man's worth? What I dislike is the fact that he purveys opium and vice down in The Red Chamber. I often spend my time treating the effects they have on his customers. Opium fuddles the mind and brain, and venereal disease rots the nether regions."

He straightened his hat and added: "And that goes for both sexes."

Fred Garvey chuckled. "Sounds funny when you say it like that, Doc." He shrugged. "But you know what Dogleg City is like. Every town has a part of it that caters to the baser instincts. I don't know if our Wolf Creek is better or worse than any other cattle or railroad town." He sucked air between his teeth. "All I know is that the law has to keep a close eye on things. We saw Sheriff Satterlee and Deputy Pennycuff head down there half an hour ago. The marshal and me are just heading down there as well. He's going to call in on *Soo Chow* hisself."

He beamed, then quickly added, "Professionally, you understand. We have to nip any trouble in the bud." He sighed. "And while he does, I have the pleasure of doing the rounds of Tent City."

Sam Gardner smoothed his goatee with the edge of

an elegantly manicured forefinger. "Law-keeping is a serious business, Doctor. Just the same as your own occupation."

Logan had previously wondered about Sam Gardner's ethics as a law officer, and his eyes narrowed a little. He suspected that his purpose in visiting Tsu Chiao may have more to do with collecting a percentage of the profits for ensuring that the opium den was left alone by the law, than to check for any misdemeanors. However, if the marshal detected any such suspicion in Logan's eyes he did not show it. He returned his gaze unblinkingly.

"Of course," Logan said. "I understand how important the law is, and how seriously you law enforcers take your jobs. Good morning, gentlemen."

He tipped his hat to them, then set off across the street. He made for a plain fronted building with steamed-up windows. A large sign above the door proclaimed it to be LI'S LAUNDRY.

Beneath it—in red calligraphic painting—the same thing was more mysteriously, and more impressively, written in Chinese:

中国洗衣店

A bell jangled as Logan pushed open the door and found himself in the steamy atmosphere. Through the steam, he could see Jing Jing, the Li family's pretty daughter, standing behind a counter talking to a young woman with corn yellow hair wearing a blue bonnet.

"Why, Doctor Munro, what a pleasant—" began the young woman before spotting his blood stained shirt.

"Miss Haselton, this is an unexpected pleasure, meeting you again so soon. Did you enjoy your supper with Bill Torrance at Isabella's Restaurant last night?"

Ann Haselton was the local schoolteacher. Her cheeks suffused with color, and Logan immediately felt he had spoken out of turn. He could see that she was embarrassed, which was rather endearing. Most folk had sensed that she had set her sights on Bill Torrance, the enigmatic owner of the Wolf Creek Livery Stable. He decided that an immediate change of conversation was called for.

"But shouldn't you be getting to the schoolhouse for the start of lessons?" he asked as he put his bag down on the floor and took off his hat.

"Oh, Mister Sublette the headmaster is going to look after both classes this morning—at least until I get back. He will be happy to talk to them for hours about his fossils and old bones," the teacher explained with a smile. "You see, I arranged to walk the four Li boys to school today. Mrs. Li has made some banners with Chinese writing on them for our school concert. The children in my class are making puppets. After we leave here with the banners, the boys and I are going to Mrs. Miller's dress shop to pick up some remnants so we can make costumes, then we'll drop in to see if Joe Nash has finished making the puppet theatre for us. Our next stop will be the *Wolf Creek Expositor*. David Appleford said he would help us print some handbills. These strong Li boys will be able to carry everything between them."

"I will get them, Miss Haselton," said Jing Jing with a little curtsy. "I apologize for their lateness. My father would scold them if he saw how they have kept you waiting."

Once she had gone, Logan and Ann Haselton passed some further pleasantries without any further mention of

Bill Torrance. Without going into details about the birth of the Blunkett twins, Logan explained how his shirt had gotten so covered in blood.

The door behind the counter opened, and Jing Jing returned, followed by three progressively smaller boys all dressed in neatly-pressed blue tunics, just like hers.

"And here is your laundry order, Doctor Munro," she said, handing him a basket with the Li's Chinese Laundry sign neatly attached.

"Thank you, Jing Jing. But what do you think about this?" Logan asked, taking off his jacket. "Will your father be able to clean the blood off this shirt?"

Before she could reply, there came the sound of a youngster singing cheerfully, then a fourth Chinese boy appeared, a full head shorter than the next smallest. It was Chang, the Li family's youngest child. He took one look at Logan's gory chest, then screamed in wide-eyed horror.

"Aiyee! Murder!" he cried. "Somebody hurt the doctor!"

His face went pale and his eyes rolled upward as his legs seemed to crumple beneath him. He was only stopped from falling and bumping his head by Ann Haselton's quick movement.

Logan immediately helped her to lay the boy down, much to his older brothers' glee.

"Chang is a baby!" said one of his brothers, and the others began to giggle.

"Hush! Hush!" came a sharp voice from behind the counter, and Mrs. Li appeared. She was dressed in a tunic with a large apron. In her gloved hand she held a heavy flatiron. Her eyes widened in alarm as she saw her son on the floor, with the teacher and the blood-splattered town doctor leaning over him. She lay the flatiron down and quickly knelt beside them, her face concerned. "So sorry, Doctor Munro and Miss Haselton. My little Chang very sensitive."

Logan cursed himself for being the cause of the child's faint. He knew Chang well, having delivered the boy himself not long after he first settled in Wolf Creek. Chang had always been a frail, nervous child, but his smile was infectious and everyone liked the little fellow.

Suddenly, a small white mouse popped its head out of the top pocket of Chang's tunic. It wrinkled its nose and looked from side to side, then made a dash for freedom. It was followed by another from a pocket in his pants.

Ann Haselton saw them and immediately jumped up and backed into a corner, tugging on her skirts as she did so. She gasped in horror.

"We will get them, Miss!" cried one of the brothers, and together, the boys scuttled about, giving chase to the mice.

Logan ignored them. Her opened his bag and pulled out a bottle of smelling salts, then wafted it under the boy's nose. Almost immediately, Chang's eyes flickered and his nose wrinkled as the salts did their job. Logan prudently pulled on his coat to cover his shirt.

As Chang started to come round, Logan chided himself. *Poor child!* What a fool he had been to show the blood-soaked shirt when youngsters were around. No little kid should have to see a mess of blood like that. And certainly, not a sensitive boy like Li Chang. Especially not on a beautiful morning like this.

Yet, although the sight of blood had caused Chang to faint, the experience did not bother him. He sat up and grinned at the sight of his brothers pursuing his mice.

"Give them to me!" he cried as two of his brothers presented them to him by their tails. "Not like that. They don't like it."

"Chang likes his animals. I think he likes them better than his brothers sometimes," Mrs. Li said with a shy smile. "Sorry if the mice upset you, Miss Haselton."

The teacher recovered herself and shrugged her shoulders with embarrassment. She turned to Logan.

"You—you won't say anything to Bill Torrance about me being frightened of mice, will you, Doctor Munro? He loves animals and he might think I was just a silly woman. I can't help it, but mice just make me squirm."

Logan smiled and shook his head. "Not a word from me. A breach of confidence would be against the Hippocratic Oath."

****

After a change of shirt and a breakfast of bacon and eggs washed down by several cups of coffee at Ma's Café, Logan had opened up his office and settled down at his big roll-top desk to await his first patients of the day. Ordinarily, he would see about twenty or so in the morning before setting off on a walking round of Wolf Creek and Dogleg City. Later on, he would head out of town to visit the ranches or homesteads as needed.

While he waited, he looked over his notes for the monograph he was writing, *The Use of Tincture of Love Vine (Clematis virginiana) in the Treatment of Gonorrhea, Gleet and Chancre in a Kansas Cowtown.*

He glanced over at his medicine mixing table with its myriad of bottles of colored liquids, jars of powders, pestle and mortar and the small vat which he used to prepare the tincture that, so far, had proven to be at least as efficacious in treating venereal disease as the standard treatment with mercurial ointment.

"I wonder how many ladies of the night or their clients I'll be treating today?" he mused.

His mind strayed back through time, to other offices and past patients of other races. And inevitably, as his gaze wandered over the walls to his framed degree and his citation for the Crimean and Turkish Medals from the Crimean War, and to the picture of Helen and himself on their wedding day in Lucknow, surrounded by his comrades from the British East India Company Army and Helen's lady friends, he felt the old pangs of loneliness and desolation. He relived the attack as he and Helen had returned to Lucknow one evening during the early days of the Indian Mutiny. Helen screaming and clutching her young charges to her while he emptied his Beaumont-Adams revolver into three turbaned, charging rebels. He had saved her from that, but not from the malaria that followed the cholera outbreak among the surviving garrison.

He reached for his meerschaum pipe and stuffed tobacco into its bowl from his battered, old oilskin pouch. A smoke would calm his nerves.

****

Emory Charleston mopped his brow with a kerchief, stuffed it into the back pocket of his canvas trousers, then put the last hard heft on the axle wrench to the left rear axle nut, and that job was done. He pulled the kerchief from his back pocket and again mopped the sweat off his wide forehead and the back of his thick neck.

All the iron tires had been retightened and axel stubs replaced on farmer Derrick McCain's dray, but now it would be good for at least another year's bouncing along rutted roads with a two thousand-pound load of corn or other produce aboard. As was his custom, Emory meandered completely around the wagon, carefully checking all the fittings, secretly admiring his work. It had only been ten years that he'd been out of the fields, doing the work of a free man.

Thanks to Mr. Lincoln, it was no longer necessary for him to worry about not having manumission papers—which he'd never had, as he'd earned his freedom ten years ago by applying the hard hickory handle of a hoe to the back of overseer Augustus St. Germain's almost equally hard head, then outrunning a dozen Louisiana redbone hounds for two days and a night until he could launch himself into a roiling over-the-bank Mississippi. The river's condition had saved him, as it made him a very hard follow—all riverside roads were awash belly deep, impassable even to a horsebacker. By the time St. Germain's kinfolk could launch boats, Emory was miles downriver—munching fruit, coasting along in the high water astride an uprooted apple tree, as comfortable as baby Moses had been in that reed basket.

His woman and knee-high girl child both dead of the yellow fever, there was nothing but fear to hold him to his masters, and he'd managed to quell that emotion long ago. And hearing that slaves were being freed, or hot-footing it for freedom all over the south, he decided to take his leave of the slave life.

He'd been three months finding his way back upriver, all the way up the Mississippi to the Missouri, then up it to Kansas, where he strode west, thinking California a fine destination. But he settled into Kansas, where there seemed to be lots of work for one willing. He made friends with other folks of color and even a few not, and soon learned whom to befriend and whom to fight shy of. And after years there doing odd jobs, dodging Redlegs up to and even after the great war of rebellion was over, he'd heard of work to the south in a booming railroad town. Work there came to him by way of a blacksmith who only seemed to judge a man by the amount of work he could do—even though the smith had worn General Lee's colors. Emory could work like two men, and stayed on with Angus "Spike" Sweeney.

He'd never looked back after putting that hickory to good work alongside the overseer's head-bone, except for many times during the war while watching for border ruffians and slave catchers.

As fate would have it, his new overseer soon came to be his partner—although they didn't advertise it about town. Work and pay had gotten short, so Emory worked on for a share. There were many who'd take great umbrage with a man of color being partner to a white man, particularly to one who'd worn the butternut and fought with the Davis Guards. Emory and Angus had long ago agreed not to discuss the relative merits of gray and blue, nor their financial association. It was an easy chore as Angus Sweeney, known as Spike to his friends, hardly said a word to anyone about anything. He was silent as an iceberg, and some thought as cold, but Emory knew better. He knew Spike well enough, after years of bending hot iron elbow to elbow and shoeing knot-headed horses shoulder to shoulder, horses who'd as soon kick you into next week. He knew a better friend couldn't be found—white, black, yellow or brown. Spike Sweeney had something engraved into a timber over the door to the shop, something that came from the South—in fact, it was reputed to have been engraved on General Lee's sword. Strangely enough, it was something Em believed with heart and soul...*Help Yourself and God Will Help You.*

Em had few friends in Wolf Creek. Many of the newer town folk were southern sympathizers and thought little of any man of color, whereas most of the citizens who had lived there longer had been the sort of Unionists who had opposed the enslavement of black people on principle, but didn't necessarily want to be seen speaking to one on the street. At least Emory knew where he stood with the Texan cowboys and assorted ex-Rebs. Most of the blacks in town at any given time, on the other hand, were migrant cowboys or railroad workers. Sometimes Em shared a drink with George Alberts, who'd also escaped slavery and now owned the leather shop, at Asa's saloon down in Dogleg City—but that was a very rough place. Asa's patrons, generally, were not the sort of company Emory preferred to keep. Em's best friend, Charley Blackfeather, was half-black, and half-Seminole, and Charley didn't spend a lot of time in town. But he, like Angus 'Spike' Sweeney, was a friend to have, and Em would hate to have either of them as enemy. They'd both proven many times they could be fearsome to their foes.

Satisfied with his work, Emory moved across the shop to a scuttlebutt and scooped up a ladle full of cool water, drank it dry, then ladled up another and poured it down the back of his neck. Felt damn good, as his thick neck was knotted from throwing around five foot high rear wagon wheels. He looked to where his partner worked, thinking he'd take him a ladle of the cool drink, but Angus was concentrating on the fine work at hand, and Emory knew he wouldn't want to be interrupted.

Emory smiled to himself. Angus was equally his tall, but only half his weight. Where Emory's arms were the size of many a man's thigh, Angus was long and lean for a smithy—but those arms were strong as oak hogshead barrel staves. Where Emory was a mite slow to move, a plow horse, Angus was a racehorse; where Emory was slow to anger, Angus had a short fuse. They made good partners in many ways, even if Angus was a bloody Rebel, a Texican, and an Anglican converted to Lutheran.

Emory had only worked under Angus's tutelage for a short while before he figured that Angus had fought, in what many Southerners called the "recent unpleasantness," for family, honor, and home, and not for the sham-honor of one man owning another. Even Angus's father had not condoned the owning of slaves— if Angus could be believed, and Emory had yet to find him to exaggerate, much less lie—and had given many a Negra his manumission. Most of those men had stayed on the Sweeney farm, working harder than they'd ever worked as slaves. Some even saved enough to buy relatives from slave owners, with Nigel Sweeney, Angus' father, acting in their stead as purchaser. The father had come from the old country, and Scotland and England had outlawed slavery decades ago. It had taken a while to worm that out of the quiet-spoken Angus, but after a year or two of working together, with Emory as an employee, Emory came to understand him and even admire him. And when Angus fell on hard times, Emory worked for beans and bacon, shared with Angus out of the same pot. They both used the same privy and washbasin, and both slept in the shop. Em worked until he had enough back wages coming to buy into the place in lieu of receiving the cash, luckily just before the business turned. It gave Emory a flush of pride when he thought of it; he had taken the chains off his own feet, and was now part owner of a forge, not only a free man but a blacksmith and a farrier (Angus was forever reminding customers that the two are not the same—blacksmiths work iron, farriers shoe horses.)

It did niggle at him that Angus always wore that damn Confederate kepi, with some fancy medal attached above its eyeshade. One of these days, Emory was going to slip it into the forge, and it would no longer be a bone of contention. Of course, he'd remove the medal first, as Angus seemed to put great stock in the piece of brass.

Emory turned his attention to a wagon tongue that needed its fittings re-welded.

****

Angus looked over and smiled to himself. He knew it would have taken him another two hours to finish the dray wagon had it been him rather than Em doing the work; damned if Em wasn't getting to the point he could outwork the senior partner. That was a hell of a note, but then he could have worse trouble. In fact, it was music to his eyes and ears.

To Angus Sweeney, the generally perceived lone proprietor of Sweeney's, the ring of a four-pound hammer on anvil, swage block, or mandrel was as beautiful as the melody he once heard emanating from the stage door of the Opera House in St. Louis. Of course, he'd just finished off a bottle of Black Widow hooch and was face-down in the alley at the time, but the strains from the violins and cellos, and the voice of a Jenny Lind imitator who was a Nightingale in her own right, stuck in his mind to this day. But, to be truthful, it was his own music he preferred even over that heard through the back door—his was the music of good honest work, and resultant tires, barrel hoops, shovels, hoes, axes, and rigging that would outlast any who didn't mistreat them. Iron on iron, ringing in regular four-four time, was the echoing melody of a man's sinew, muscle, and bone—making hard metal bend to his will.

At the moment, he was busy on the mandrel. He'd formed a half-dozen cinch keepers and was now forming the circular side as the iron was cooling after being welded into the rough shape that would serve to bind latigo to saddle after George Alberts, the saddle maker, stitched them in place on one of the fine saddles he made. Before he'd started on McCain's dray, Em had just completed rebuilding some hinges on Albert's draw-down table, and Albert was eager to get back on the saddles and get them shipped off. This was fine work, as fine as that of a tinsmith, not the bone-jarring pounding necessary for forming wagon tires or ax heads or railroad spikes, which he often had done for miners who wanted ore car rails snaking into the holes they cut into the mountainside. In fact, that was how he got his nickname, Spike. He'd worked sixteen hours a day for a good long while, fulfilling a contract for a thousand such rail spikes, much to the chagrin of others who wanted some work out of him. They thought it a derogatory name, but he kind of liked it.

The mines were a place he hoped he'd never have to work. He hated the thought of living his life in a rat hole as much as many hated the thought of working hammer and tongs next to white iron while a forge at your back hiked the temperature in the shop well above the hundred-degree mark, even when the horse troughs outside got a shimmer of ice on their surface from a Kansas norther. But he should never have to become a mine rat, as his business was doing just fine, enough to support both himself and his partner. And he liked fire and iron.

And they did fine, he and Emory. One always trying to outwork the other was a good basis for a business, and a partnership.

At first glance, the shop might fool many as, if not for the forge, it looked as much like a ship's chandlery as an ironsmith's abode. It had rigging that recalled the block and tackle of many a ship, rigging used to move heavy iron and wheel-less wagons around the space. This was because Angus had spent many an early year aboard ship, both on the river and in the Gulf of Mexico, learning the trade of a smithy while pounding out chains, anchors, rigging, connections, repairing boilers, and even doing fine decorative work—fancy hatch hinges, latches, and running lights—of both sailing and steam vessels. He had also become a master with rope rigging and could tie a blight, crown knot, or barrel hitch with the best of them, but Wolf Creek had little use for decorative knots, and the hangman's noose was about as fancy as he'd been called upon to preform since he'd settled here.

Angus and Emory alike were happy to fill their days with simple work. They had each had more than enough excitement in their lives, in one way or another, to last them. Wolf Creek was just the town for both of them, they told each other more than once. On a summer day

like this—peaceful and quiet, so long as one stayed north
of Dogleg City—that seemed truer than ever.

CHAPTER TWO

Wil Marsh, Wolf Creek's photographer, had felt like death warmed over when he had woken up. A late night at the Wolf's Den had significantly lightened his wallet. He was not sure which had been more responsible; Ira Breedlove's rot-gut whiskey, or the house gambler Preston Vance's skill with the cards. He had no doubt that the whiskey had given him the gut ache and caused his eyes to feel as if they had been taken out, rubbed in the dirt and stuck back in again. He was less sure whether Vance was the fine-skilled Virginian gambler that he claimed to be or just a highly competent card sharp.

After a retching session and a hasty ablution, he headed off to his studio. He had thought of going past Li Wong's laundry to see if he could try a little flirtation with the beautiful exotic Jing Jing, whom he lusted after. Feeling as bad as he did, he reckoned he might not be at his most appealing, so he made his way across 'Useless Grant' Street, and on toward Birdie's General Store on North Street where he bought tobacco and a fresh supply of coffee. Then he went across the street to the telegraph office.

Dave Maynard, the telegrapher, was a man of few words. He dealt with Marsh's telegram to Wichita for more chemicals for his photographic studio with silent efficiency. It amused Marsh that a man whose work

31

revolved around communication could be so shy that he barely ever said a word to anyone. He reckoned that was why the guy seemed to be a confirmed bachelor. Yet, Marsh's hangover was making him feel cantankerous enough to want to jibe some conversation out of the reticent telegrapher.

"I see you got lots of burns on your arms," he remarked. He pulled back a sleeve and showed his own arm. "I get chemical burns in my line of work, as well." He smirked internally, for his burns had been from a time in his past when he, too, had been a telegraph operator and had to tend to the lead-acid batteries.

Dave Maynard looked up and blushed. He had not really talked to the photographer before. He wasn't the sort that he naturally took to. He thought that Wil Marsh was shifty, and always seemed to be on the lookout for something. He guessed he had a past he didn't want to reveal…kind of like half the folk who had settled in Wolf Creek.

"Yes, folks don't realize how the acid in these batteries burns."

Marsh persisted and forced conversation, all the time keeping an eye on what was going on outside. He noted everything. He spotted Mason Wright carrying a tray of bread and pies, presumably heading toward the Imperial Hotel. He saw the tall figure of Derrick McCain stride past. And he observed the wagon with a tarpaulin covering its load being hauled along North Street by a mule. A horse was tethered to the back and trotted along behind it. He didn't recognize the driver, a surly-looking fellow with lank red hair and a cigar hanging languidly from the corner of his mouth.

"Now, me, I plan to make enough money here in

Wolf Creek, and then I'm headed East. I just need to take me some really sensational photographs to sell to some of those fancy newspapers and magazines."

Dave Maynard nodded his head in the direction of the window. "What about the *Wolf Creek Expositor*? David Appleford is making that newspaper of his really sell in these parts."

Marsh was non-committal. He had not exactly hit it off with the newsman so far. Instead, he resumed his discourse about eastern magazines and his plans for the future.

A few moments later, he saw a second wagon pass and turn onto Fourth Street. Strangely, as soon as he had turned the corner, he began turning the mule round as if to come back on itself.

"What's that fool think he's doing?" Marsh sneered. "He's going to get stuck."

They watched as the driver jumped down, circled the wagon and drew back a tarpaulin. He fiddled with something in the back of the wagon, then took out his cigar, blew on it and applied it to the contents of the wagon. Moments later they saw flames, and then thick smoke started to curl upward.

"Shit! What the hell is he doing?" Marsh exclaimed.

From a couple of streets away came the sound of a gunshot. Then, as Marsh and Maynard stared in horror, the man drew his gun from its holster and circled the wagon again. The mule was snorting in alarm and trying to move away from the burning load behind it.

The man raised his gun and shot the animal between the eyes.

****

Jim Danby took a final glance at his watch then stowed it inside his vest. He ran the back of his hand against the three days' growth of stubble on his cheek and stretched himself in the saddle. He was a lean, rangy man of about thirty with a ready, toothy smile and cruel eyes. A product of the War, he and his men had ridden with Quantrill and reveled in the Lawrence Raid. Since then, under his leadership, the Danby gang had become one of the most successful and feared gangs in the West. They had parlayed their wartime skills into bank-robbing. And in Danby's eyes, they were the best, because *he* was the best. Planning and ruthless execution were his tenets.

"Any moment now," he said to Wes Hammond, his lieutenant and comrade of almost ten years.

Wes Hammond nodded dispassionately. Unlike Danby, he was not given to smiling, unless he was doing what he was best at—hurting people. He was about the same age and build as his boss, although with his longer hair, petulant lips and clean-shaven face he looked somewhat younger. He nodded and pulled his hat firmly down on his head.

Danby put a hand on the pommel of his saddle and turned round to face the twenty mounted men. They had gathered out of sight of the town in the trees that fringed the boulders on the other side of Wolf Creek. "Okay boys, we go in as planned, as soon as we hear the first two shots. We cross the ford and hit the town. I'll take the first column down the main street. Wes will lead the other down the first left, then along Lincoln Street. You all know the layout."

Wes turned in his saddle. He drew out his beloved .42 Le Mat cap and ball black powder revolver. Not made for fast drawing, it was virtually a one-man artillery piece. With nine shots in its cylinder for shooting from the regular barrel, it also had an 18-gauge shotgun barrel beneath for its tenth shot. He hefted it in his hand and raised it. It had been a popular piece among various elements of the Confederacy. It took time to load—but as a killing piece, he was proud of it. And on a raid such as this, once he had discharged every round, he had his Navy Colts to fall back on.

"We are all armed to the teeth. This will go as smooth as silk. We're going to divide up into threes and fours. Each group will take one of the sections of the two main streets. Bates and Milton will already have cut the town in two and contained the law, so one man from each group will cover all the alleys and side streets in his section. If anyone so much as pops their head into an alley, discourage them. If they won't stay discouraged—kill them."

Danby grinned. Although Wes had needed to be shown who was the master in their early days, he liked to think that he had inculcated and refined a streak of ruthlessness in him. "Ketch and Jackson, you two know what you have to do?"

A stocky young rider at the back grinned. "Sure we know, boss. We shoot every damned horse we see."

Danby clicked his tongue "Good man!" He pulled up his bandanna and signaled for the gang members to do likewise.

Two separate shots rang out from different parts of the town, and thick smoke started to rise into the blue sky. Moments later the Danby gang hit the ford over Wolf Creek and galloped toward the town.

****

Bill Torrance, owner of the Wolf Creek Livery Stable, was looking forward to an easy day, the first one he'd had in several weeks. The last of the trail herds had been shipped three days previously. With the Texas cowhands who drove those herds now headed back home his stable was more than half empty, the only horses in his care those of his regular clients.

By eight-thirty, Bill had already completed the heavy chores of the day. The horses were fed, watered, and most turned into the corral. All the stalls had been mucked out, the soiled bedding and manure dumped into the ever-growing pile out back. While Bill wasn't bothered by the smell of horse manure, in fact rather enjoying its earthy pungency, the fly-attracting, odiferous mound was a bone of contention between himself and the pastor and congregation of the nearby church.

"Now that you're all nice and shiny, reckon it's time I wash up too, Cholla," Bill told his big paint gelding, giving the horse's bay and white splotched coat a final swipe of the currycomb. "You wait here while I get my stuff."

Bill's horse snorted, then nuzzled his shoulder in reply. Cholla was rarely secured in his stall, mostly having the run of the stable, and a small corral of his own. He'd been with Bill for years, the man and equine having a deep bond, far beyond the usual relationship between a rider and horse. Bill himself had an almost mystical connection with horses. People had always said Bill seemed to speak horses' language. If fact, Bill would be the first to admit he preferred the company of horses to that of most people he'd met, and understood equines far better than humans.

Bill headed into the small room at the back of the stable which was his living quarters. He removed a bar of soap, washcloth, towel, and his shaving kit from a battered five-drawer chest, then headed outside, to the back of the stable, Cholla following. He had an old horse trough there which served as a washbasin, along with a mirror hanging from the barn wall. Bill placed his gear on the bench alongside the trough, then peeled off his shirt, revealing a puckered bullet scar high on the right side of his chest, along with an old saber scar which ran diagonally across his belly, from just under his left breast almost to his right hip. He ducked his head in the trough, soaking his unruly thatch of sandy hair. Cholla nuzzled insistently at Bill's shoulder, nickering.

"Will you cut it out, horse?" Bill chided. "I know you're jealous, just 'cause I had supper with Ann Haselton last night, rather'n you."

Bill had been an enigma to the citizens of Wolf Creek since his arrival over a year back. He'd ridden into town with no gun on his hip or rifle on his saddle, and since then had given no indication he'd ever touched a weapon. He bought the livery—which was in an advanced state of disrepair—from old Walt Corriher, then spent almost all his time fixing up the place and caring for his equine charges. Except for occasional visits to the Eldorado Saloon, and his regular meals at Ma's Café, Bill basically kept to himself. He'd never even been seen entering Abby Potter's "Boarding House", to be entertained by one of her girls, nor, to anyone's knowledge, had he partaken of the services of the many prostitutes available in Dogleg City.

"Doggone it, I said cut it out," Bill repeated, when

Cholla placed his muzzle into the small of Bill's back and shoved. "If I want to go out with a lady, I'm gonna do just that. Besides, I'd imagine Miss Ann has much prettier legs than yours, pard."

A smile played across Bill's face, and his gray eyes sparkled at the memory of last evening. Ann Haselton, Wolf Creek's schoolteacher, had been dropping not-so-subtle hints for quite some time she was interested in getting to know him better. After months, Bill had finally worked up the courage to ask her to supper, and she'd accepted. Instead of Bill's usual place, Ma's, they'd gone to Isabella's Restaurant, where Antonio, the owner, had provided a sumptuous meal. From Isabella's they went to the Imperial Hotel for pie and coffee. Everything was perfectly proper, of course, in keeping with Ann's position as schoolmarm. When Bill escorted her back to her small cottage on Lincoln Street, two doors from the schoolhouse, their goodbye had been a handshake, not a kiss. He'd also made sure plenty of people saw Ann go inside, alone.

While Bill washed and shaved, Cholla kept nuzzling his shoulders and nipping his ears, despite Bill's threats to turn him into dog food. When Bill bent over the trough to rinse the shaving lather from his face, Cholla clamped his teeth onto Bill's belt, lifted him into the air, and dumped him unceremoniously into the trough. Bill emerged, spluttering, and muttering various uncomplimentary oaths about Cholla's ancestry. He turned at the sound of raucous laughter.

"Hey, Bill, why the devil are you takin' a bath? It ain't anywhere near Saturday," Jed Stevens called. Like Bill, Stevens, head wrangler for the Lazy H Ranch, had a special affinity for horses. He was the only person in

Wolf Creek who Bill would call a close friend.

"Wasn't my idea, it was Cholla's," Bill answered. "I think he's jealous 'cause I had supper with Ann Haselton last night."

"Well, you're the one who turned that animal into a biscuit-eater," Jed replied. "You spoil that horse."

"I know, but he deserves it," Bill replied. "I'd trust him over most of the people I've known, no question. Besides, you spoil your Rojo every bit as much."

"Boy howdy, I can't argue with you there, on either point," Jed agreed. "Never mind your horse, though. Half the town's buzzin' about you bein' seen having supper with the schoolteacher. So, tell me about last night."

"We had supper, that's all. Ann's a real—"

Bill stopped short, as the sound of gunshots and pounding hooves shattered the morning.

"What the hell?" Jed exclaimed. He pulled his Navy Colt from its holster. "Better see what that's all about."

He and Bill headed for North Street on the run.

****

The jangle of a bell from the outer waiting room stopped Logan from lighting his pipe, and with a shrug of resignation, he stood and crossed the room. A bit of work was needed to help him stave off the tiredness after his night's work and the melancholic mood that was never too far away when he thought of his Helen.

He opened the door to find himself confronting the intimidating, unsmiling figure of Charley Blackfeather. The scout was taller than Logan by a couple of inches and weighed about two hundred pounds of almost pure muscle. Charley's father had been a runaway slave, and his mother was a Seminole. He had the proud, handsome features of both races. His raven black hair hung down his back in a single long braid. Eschewing a shirt, he was dressed in a blue cavalry slouch cap adorned with a single crow feather, a black vest and canvas pants. His feet were encased in high-topped beaded moccasins, and about his waist was a veritable armory of weaponry. He carried an Army Colt, a Bowie knife, and a steel tomahawk that Logan had once seen him hurl to decapitate a rat at thirty paces.

"For you," he said, holding out a small sack that seemed to be moving, as if it contained something alive. "Green frogs. They're good for pounding into hog fat with some of the herbs I brought last time. They'll cure any ulcer."

Logan took the bag from the Indian scout and opened it. A small green frog instantly leaped out, but Charley Blackfeather caught it in mid-air and deposited it back in the bag.

"Thanks, Charley," Logan said, tying the bag and pointing to his consulting room. "Come and have a coffee."

"No," Charley returned taciturnly. "I have business with Casto Haston at the tannery." He pointed through the window to his horse which was hitched outside, and at the load of hides strapped to the back of his saddle alongside his bow and the scabbard containing his '66 Winchester Yellowboy.

"You just make some of that green frog ointment. You'll find it's much better than anything else you got. It's an old Seminole remedy that my mama used on me many a time. It works on gunshot wounds, too."

Logan took a pragmatic approach to medicine and

was willing to try out all manner of the Indian remedies that Charley Blackfeather supplied him with. He was not too sure about using green frogs, though.

Just then, Ann Haselton passed the window with the four Li boys following her in a line, each carrying a basket. Logan guessed that they were now on their way to the newspaper office. Little Chang was bringing up the rear, a broad grin on his face. They all waved as they passed. Logan was sure that Li Chang would have been delighted to see the bagful of green frogs, but probably less enamored at the fate that Charley Blackfeather proposed for them.

Logan and Charley chatted for a few minutes more, and then Charley turned and reached for the doorknob. He stopped and stood still, sniffing the air.

"Something is burning!" he said.

Logan smelled it too.

Then there was the sound of a gun. It was followed by another from somewhere further off. Almost immediately, there was the cadence of galloping hooves.

The sudden sound of a child's scream sent a shiver down Logan's spine. He immediately knew who it was, for he had heard the sound not long before.

Charley Blackfeather pulled the door open and he and Logan rushed out. They saw a burning wagon belching thick black smoke skewed across halfway up the street. A dead mule lay before it.

"What in blazes?" Logan began.

Then a gun fired, and a bullet sent them dashing back into the office. From all over town came startled voices and cries. The noise of horses' hooves pounding could be heard and then the noise of more gunfire. Lots of it.

"*It's a raid!*" shouted Logan, rushing into his

consulting room and grabbing his bag.

Charley stopped him as he tried to go back into the waiting room.

"If there is shooting, there will be wounded. I'll be needed."

"You won't be needed *dead*, doctor. Go the back way."

Together they left Logan's place via a back window, and gingerly skirted round the back of the office.

"You there, lay down that gun!" they heard a voice cry from Second Street. "I'm Deputy Marshal Garvey and I order you—"

There was a gunshot, then a scream.

As they hurried round the side of the office, they saw Fred Garvey's body lying in the dirt, blood gushing from a chest wound.

"You mangy dog!" cried Marshal Sam Gardner, running toward the blazing wagon, firing both guns through the smoke.

Another shot rang out and the marshal was hit. Blood spurted from his left leg, and he collapsed on his side. More bullets dug up clouds of earth around him, and he crawled sidewinder fashion, dragging his shot leg, to the cover of a horse trough.

"You got a gun, Munro?" Charley Blackfeather asked.

Logan opened his bag and drew out his Beaumont-Adams revolver. "I carried this through three wars. It is a fine weapon." He hefted it in his firm surgeon's hand. "And I can use it."

Charley gave the curtest of acknowledgments. "We need to get past this gunman. If you pin him down, I'll see if I can get around in back of him."

Logan obliged. Intermittently, he peered round the corner of the office and discharged a shot. With each one, a returned shot gouged out part of the wall. Whoever was firing from the other side of the grisly barricade knew how to shoot.

Suddenly, there was a dull thud and a harrowing scream that went on and on, as if someone was in mortal agony. Then, abruptly, the noise stopped.

"Logan!" Charley Blackfeather called.

Logan peered round the corner, and through the smoke, saw Charley Blackfeather gesturing to him. In one hand he held his metal tomahawk and in the other, his big Bowie knife. Both were dripping with blood.

"Maybe you should take care of the marshal," he shouted. And without another word, he turned and disappeared into the smoke.

****

Masked, armed men had galloped into Wolf Creek and seemed to be everywhere on both North and Lincoln Streets. They had pinned the town down, having shot mules and set fire to wagons that blocked off both Fourth and Second Streets. Already, a pall of acrid smoke had drifted down the streets, adding to the confusion.

As the gang rode in, they had split into smaller groups, and while some had dismounted and systematically pillaged businesses and shops, others had either remained on horseback and raced back and forth between the connecting streets or dismounted and taken up positions where they could cut off any resistance.

The raid was carried out with military precision, the effect being much as Danby's crew would have wished.

43

Most of the townspeople were panicked.

Two of the gunmen rode up the streets shooting at close range all the horses that were tied to the various hitching rails. The horses, sensing their danger, were panicking as well, with much snorting, squealing and screaming.

"You damned murdering dogs!" cried Slim Tabner, one of the tannery workers, running down Lincoln Street with an old Dragoon revolver. He stopped as soon as he came within range of one of the mounted men, took aim and fired. He hit the outlaw in the chest, and he was thrown sideward, landing in the dust in front of Wright's Bakery. Immediately, one of the dismounted gunmen fired back, the bullet hitting Slim in the head and splattering blood and brain matter on the ground behind him.

At the other end of the town, Jim Danby, Wes Hammond and their men had converged on the Wolf Creek Savings and Loan. Melvin Lohorn, the owner, had been startled by all the noise and the sudden appearance of five armed men who had kicked and barged their way in and immediately shot down Hank Jones and Jeremiah Barnes, the two tellers on duty. Three of the men had then forced staff and customers onto the floor while the leader had made Melvin open the safe, himself. The other kept a watch at the door.

Once they had loaded up their saddlebags, for good measure they knocked out Allen Cook, the accountant, and Melvin Lohorn with the butts of their weapons. Then they departed, firing a few shots into the walls above the heads of the prostrate customers.

"Anyone who makes any move to come after us will get to lie down permanently!" Danby growled.

****

At the first sound of gunshots, Bill Torrance and his friend Jed Stevens had left the livery and run to North Street. The sight of a small army galloping along North Street toward them, and the other riders heading off down Fifth Street, left them in no doubt as to what was happening. It was a raid on the town, but most likely the main aim was to hit the bank.

"Holy smoke!" exclaimed Jed, clenching his Navy Colt. "Let's hope Marshal Gardner and Sheriff Satterlee and their deputies are close by. I'm going to see what's happening."

"They're shooting up the whole place," gasped Bill. "I'm going to make sure Ann and the school kids all stay off the street."

"You watch yourself, buddy," Jed said. "Everybody knows you never carry a gun, but these yahoos might not care."

As Jed ran down one alley, Bill turned and darted down another, then dashed across North Street into the school.

Marcus Sublette, the headmaster, was looking out the window when Bill rushed in. He had already shepherded the children to the other end of the classroom and forbidden them to allow their curiosity to get the better of them.

"Where's Miss Haselton?" Bill asked in surprise.

"She—she hasn't come in yet. She was running some errands with the Li Children first. It's for the—"

Full of fear for Ann, Bill dashed out and almost ran into Derrick McCain, who was running up an alley toward North Street.

"Have you seen Ann Haselton?" Bill asked, urgently.

"Yeah, I saw her duck into the *Expositor* office with those Chinese boys. She's safe enough there."

The two men had never gotten on, having different allegiances during the War, but Bill put a hand on the younger man's shoulder and heaved a sigh of relief. He was about to say something when the sound of repeated shots from the bank rang out. Then the door flew open and a handful of gunmen charged out, each carrying a heavy saddle-bag. The leader whistled, and a moment later, a mounted raider came around the corner trailing the reins of their horses. They threw their bags over their saddles, mounted and wheeled round in readiness to make their escape.

Then, Danby spied Bill and Derrick on the other side of the street. A hard light came into his eyes. "Hey, remember this son of a bitch?" he shouted to Wes Hammond. Danby laughed mirthlessly. "This is like old-home week! Bet I kill him first!"

And, almost simultaneously, they both raised their guns and fired.

Instinctively, Bill and Derrick dived for cover. Bill hit the ground and rolled over to find the protection of a shed. Derrick dived over a trough.

Both Danby and Hammond raised their guns again, moving in for the kill.

"Shoot the bastard!" Danby cried.

But a shot rang out from close by, and they both looked round to see its source. Bill saw Jed flatten himself against the side of a building, his smoking Navy Colt in his hand. It was enough to distract Danby and Hammond, and since they could not see where the shot had come from, they took off and their men followed.

"Remember to shoot any horses. Don't want any of these Wolf Creekers following!" Danby cried.

Bill ran over to Jed. "My God! They're shooting the horses. Cholla!"

"And my Rojo!"

Together they raced along Lincoln and rounded the corner to the livery.

The first of the raiders were racing along North Street as Bill and Jed approached the livery. Rojo, Jed's beloved strawberry roan gelding, was tethered to the hitching rail in front just as Jed had left him, alongside a sorrel. Both horses were snorting and straining to get loose.

One of the five drew to a halt, pulled out his gun and shot the sorrel once in the head, and Rojo twice in the chest. The sorrel dropped dead instantly, but Rojo reeled, and then collapsed. He lay there, making a fearful noise, with his legs twitching.

"No!" cried Jed, rushing ahead. He raised his gun and fired at the raider, but missed.

The gunman made no such mistake. He shot Jed in the chest. Then, seeing Bill coming along behind him, he let off a shot at him.

Jed, feeling his life slipping away, ignored the gunman and staggered toward Rojo—who lay snorting and squealing, his eyes rolling and his great chest pumping blood out.

"Rojo," Jed sobbed. "The bastard has done for us both." And realizing that there was nothing he could do for his mount, his friend of so many years, he dropped to his knees and patted the horse's neck. Rojo nickered at the feel of his owner's hand.

"I can't stand to see you suffer, Rojo," he wheezed as

he pressed a hand to the gushing wound on his chest. He raised the gun to Rojo's head. "We'll go together, buddy!"

He fired and shuddered as his horse convulsed, then lay still. Then, with his eyes full of tears, he slumped forward over Rojo and died.

The gunman laughed and then turned in the direction of the stable and the corral beyond, where Bill had left Cholla and all his other charges.

Bill seized the opportunity, his heart racing and his mind full of nothing except the desire for revenge. He ran, grabbed the gun from Jed's dead hand, and shot the departing gunman in the back.

****

Ann and the Li children had taken refuge in the *Expositor* where the editor, David Appleford, and his printer, Piney Robbins, had done their best to keep the boys' heads down.

At last, when the shooting and the screaming of the dying horses seemed to be over and the gang all seemed to have ridden off, Piney stood up, grabbed the old Baby Dragoon pocket revolver that he kept in his desk drawer, and opened the door into the street. The sight that greeted him made him feel sick. The street was still full of smoke and the smell of powder was everywhere. A couple of businesses had caught fire or been deliberately set alight. Through the haze, he saw the carcasses of about a dozen horses lying where they had been slain as they stood tied to hitching rails. Two human bodies lay at the far end of the street.

Then he heard the noise of hooves and saw two

gunmen riding fast toward him. He took a step to the edge of the boardwalk and aimed his weapon.

The leading raider saw him and fired, his bullet going wide. Piney barely aimed, but luck was with him. The bullet caught the raider in the face and he tumbled backward overt his horse to land face up in an expanding pool of his own blood.

At that very moment, Li Chang's mice escaped from his pockets and made a concerted bid for freedom through the open door. Despite the combined cries of David Appleford and Chang's brothers, Chang chased after them, his mind numbed by the horror of all he had heard. All he wanted was to protect his precious mice. He dashed through the door into the street then stopped when he saw the bloody body of a horse lying right in front of him.

He did not see the frightened, riderless horse that had reared up as it lost its rider and then started into a gallop. It ran straight into Chang, its full weight trampling him into the ground, shattering his rib cage and instantly breaking his neck.

Ann Haselton had instinctively run out after him, then stopped and stared in horror at seeing him trampled to death. She ran to him as soon as she was able, not seeing the panicking final gunman who had started shooting at anything that moved. He shot her in the back. The bullet went straight through her heart and she fell over the dead, broken body of her charge, Li Chang.

****

Spike and Emory had both been working hammer and tong, without a word between them—which was normal—when they'd heard the sound of gunfire. Each glanced at the other, then Spike grabbed the Austrian .50 caliber he kept loaded and leaning on the ladder to the loft, and headed for the wagon doors which stood open. In seconds, he spun on his heel and yelled to his partner as he passed. "Town's under attack—least there's a hell of a gunfight going on. Grab the Spencer—I'll take the side from above, you take the front."

The north side of the blacksmith's shop looked out toward Torrance's Livery, the front toward the school. The shop was on the edge of town, not in its center, where the shots came from. It was Spike's thought that raiders, if indeed this was a raid, would be looking for anything of value, and Torrance kept some fine stock at his place. Spike, however, was more worried about his own steel gray.

He couldn't imagine them bothering the school. He was better armed than Em, and knew himself to be a better shot; after all, he'd been four years getting shot at by some of Mr. Lincoln's finest, and other than a scar across his cheekbone—and that from a blade—and a limp from a cannon blast, he was not much the worse for the wear.

Even though a lot more lead could be thrown from the Spencer, the long rifled Austrian was a much more accurate weapon at a distance, and he would lay down only fifty yards from the livery. He could put one through a button on a man's vest at that range. He'd once dropped a Yank sniper out of a hickory tree with the long Austrian, and then paced off the four hundred-and-thirty-yard shot.

As he'd suspected, and just as he got prone in the loft, two riders he didn't recognize approached the livery. To his surprise, one of them drew and head-shot a horse tied at a rail across the road from the corrals—the animal collapsed like he'd dropped a hogshead barrel.

Spike had no idea who the men were, but it didn't take more than that one gunshot to figure them up to no good—the question was, did they deserve killing? He snapped the gun to his shoulder, took a deep breath, squeezed, and shot the mount out from under the lead rider—who hit the ground on the run, caught the arm of the second, and swung up behind him. As Spike bit the end off another paper load, they disappeared behind the houses at a dead gallop.

His own horse, Hammer, a steel gray dappled gelding—cut proud enough that he still wanted to jump the fence when there was a mare on the wind—was in that livery, and he and Ham had been though a lot together. He wasn't going to see him shot down by some lowlife. Reloading, he waited for another butt-wipe to ride on the livery, but none came.

Spike did have money in the bank, and that concerned him, for raiders would surely make it their first target. But from many battles under many different conditions, he knew one thing for sure. It was better to evaluate your position, and the odds, before you set off half-cocked—to coin a particularly appropriate phrase. That is, if you wanted to stay alive.

More shots rang out from different areas of town. Either there were plenty of raiders or some damn townsfolk-fools were shooting at each other. He and Em held their ground until the shooting quieted down. Then he dismounted the ladder, bade Em to take up his position in the loft, and retrieved his shirt. He buttoned up—he normally worked bare-chested in the shop's heat—and strode out for the bank, only a block down Lincoln Street. Moving from cover to cover, keeping close to the walls of the buildings he passed, he kept a sharp eye for strangers or anyone armed.

As he neared the town's most substantial masonry building, he realized the situation was damn bad. Not only were some men shot up, but a fine young lady, the schoolmarm, Miss Ann Haselton, and a child, one of the Li children—the youngest, Spike thought—lay dead.

His throat went dry, and heat coursed his backbone.

Spike had seen enough death to last him several lifetimes and had thought he was immune to it, but the woman and the child got to him. He stopped and stared at the weeping women who bent over the prostrate bodies, and old snakes started wiggling in his belly. He hated the thought of it, but innocent blood had been spilled—and that meant that blood had to be taken.

****

Bill stood, numbed, alongside the bodies of his friend, Jed, and Jed's horse. The Danby gang had raced west along North Street and out of Wolf Creek, leaving death and destruction in its wake. Powdersmoke, mingled with the smoke from burning wagons and three blazing buildings, formed a haze which burned Bill's eyes, already filled with tears over Jed's loss. Those tears mercifully blurred his vision as he looked over the carnage on North Street. He could see the bodies of at least three people, plus those of nine or ten horses. Somewhere down the street a dog howled mournfully, undoubtedly at the loss of its master. The cries of the terrified, wounded, and dying sounded as if Satan and his legions were invading Wolf Creek. Of course Jim Danby, Wes Hammond, and Satan were one and the same to Bill.

"Cholla!"

Bill tucked Jed's pistol into the waistband of his pants, then headed inside the stable, the dead outlaw's horse following, eager to get away from the smoke and blood. Bill's vow to never again use a gun had been shattered when he saw Jed murdered, and Rojo, along with who knew how many other helpless horses, gunned down where they stood. He had acted strictly on instinct when he grabbed the gun from Jed's dying hand and shot his killer. The man had turned away from Jed and toward Bill's stable, clearly intent on killing the horses inside, then burning down the barn. There was no way Bill could let that happen. A quick bullet in the back was the only solution.

The few horses remaining in the stalls were still nervous, pacing, snorting and nickering, eyes rolling and nostrils flaring at the scent of smoke.

"Cholla!" Bill called again. His paint came charging from his corral and up to Bill. He stopped and nuzzled Bill's chest, then whickered. Bill wrapped his arms around the big gelding's neck.

"Dunno why you didn't follow me like you always do, boy, but thank God you didn't," Bill murmured. "Somethin' must've told you to stay behind. Cowboy once told me there's a saint—Francis if I recollect right— who protects animals. Guess he was watchin' over you, ol' pard. If he was, I'm sure grateful. Meantime, I'd better try and calm your friends down, then see where I can help out."

Bill was more sickened by the killing of many of Wolf Creek's horses than that of several of its residents.

After all, his thinking went, men always had a way to fight back. Horses had no such choice. They were innocent victims of man's greed and inhumanity.

Deputy Fred Garvey's horse, a blocky grulla gelding, was in the stall closest to Bill. Bill stroked its nose to soothe the frightened animal.

"Easy, Dusty," Bill whispered. "They're gone. Nothin' to worry about now."

"Bill! You in there? Sheriff Satterlee's lookin' for you. Needs you *pronto.*"

Jimmy Spotted Owl was standing in the door of the stable. The young half-Cherokee cowboy's face was streaked with gunpowder.

"Satterlee's lookin' for me? Why?" Bill questioned.

"'Cause he's gettin' up a posse, and needs horses. Gotta get on the trail of those renegades before they get too much of a jump. Sheriff wants to know how many horses you've got left."

"Tell him half a dozen, not countin' my Cholla," Bill answered.

"You'd better tell him yourself," Jimmy replied. "I've got to find Billy Below and Phil Salem. We're gonna ride with Satterlee. Whole town's riled up over all the killin's, especially little Li Chang and the schoolteacher."

Bill's heart jumped into his throat.

"You mean they killed Marcus Sublette?"

"Not Marcus Sublette. Ann Haselton."

Bill gasped. He felt like he'd just taken a Comanche lance right through his gut.

"Miss Haselton? Are you certain?"

"Saw her body myself. One of those bastards shot her right in the back."

"Jimmy, tell G.W. I'll be at his office in five

minutes."

"Bill, you don't even wear a gun," Jimmy started to protest, then stopped short, when he noticed the Colt snugged in the hostler's waistband, and the grim look in Bill's gray eyes.

"Don't matter none," Bill said.

"No, I reckon it don't," Jimmy agreed.

Once Jimmy left, Bill went to his room. He pulled open the bottom drawer of his chest and removed two boxes. The longer of these he set on top of the chest. He opened the other and removed a pair of well-oiled Navy Colts, along with a still-supple gunbelt and holsters. The bullet loops were filled with .44 Henry shells. Bill settled the belt on his hips, buckled it in place, then checked the action of the Colts before sliding them into their holsters.

Cholla was still waiting in the aisleway.

"C'mon, pardner, we've got a job to do, just like we've done before," Bill murmured to the paint.

****

Spike knew George Washington Satterlee, the sheriff, and he'd want to bring these scum suckin' pigs back to town and make a big deal out of trying and hanging them. Hell, it would probably make *Leslie's Weekly* and the lawman would be famous. But Spike had already made up his mind that these ol' boys, who'd ridden down innocent women and children, would rot out there on the trail somewhere, and their trip to burn in hell would be as short as Spike could arrange. The crows would be pickin' their eyes before many moons would pass, had he his way.

But as was his custom, he didn't mouth it, just swore

it to himself. A blood oath, for spilled blood.

He'd hoped he'd seen the end of it with the close of the war, but knew as long as there were men, there'd be killing.

He spat on the dirt street in disgust, and walked on.

And to add insult to that injury, when he got to the Wolf Creek Savings and Loan, he found his money was gone along with the rest of the town's. He'd worked hard for four years putting money in that bank—as well as, thank God, some in a tobacco can buried in his flower and vegetable garden out back of the shop. Another reason to see the crows were well fed. More importantly, more lay dead. Two young tellers, Hank Jones and Jeremiah Barnes, lay dead on the floor, blood pooling around them. Hank was a married man with a new child. Spike's mouth was so dry he couldn't work up a spit. He clamped his jaw and walked out, heading for the sheriff's office.

He waited quietly for the town fathers to get themselves pulled together, then when the first hint of posse was uttered, told them he'd return ready to ride. He went first to the livery where he kept his horse and a steamer trunk full of tack and other mementos from his time in the war, saddled Hammer, tied his two saddle holsters in place, a rifle boot on either side against the fenders. Then he went to the shop where he spent several minutes convincing Em that someone had to stay and take care of business. It wouldn't do for both of them to get shot all to hell chasing a bunch of worthless owlhoots. He dug into the steamer trunk he kept in the loft, packed his haversack, rolled a blanket, made sure his cartridge and cap box was full, and headed back to the sheriff's office to team up with the rest of the posse. Emory

Charleston watched his partner ride out, and bowed his head and took a moment to ask the good Lord to watch over him.

He left Emory with the Spenser, but shoved the long Austrian in one saddle boot, a pair of Rigdon and Ainsley Confederate Navy Colt copies in the saddle holsters, and a double barrel twelve gauge in the other boot. His saddlebags would hold two dozen brass twelve gauge shells loaded with double-aught buckshot. The Austrian would do fine for long work, the revolvers for medium, and the scattergun for close, bloody work.

When he rode up, Spence Pennycuff was waiting on the boardwalk. He eyed Spike up and down. "Hell, Sweeney, you look like you'd be ready to take on half of General Lee's army."

Spike tapped the kepi on his head. "You got the wrong side there, Spence. If there was still takin' on to do, I'd be taking on Cump Sherman's boys. But that's all behind us now. Let's get to takin' on these raiders."

Spence smiled broadly. "That's the most I think I hear'd you say since I known you, Spike."

"Well, sir, these are trying times, and talking never got no row hoed or nag shoed."

"C'mon in, Spike," Spence said. "Sheriff's got a few directions for us, I'm sure."

****

The whole town was sickened at the sights and the news of the lives lost. No one's worst nightmare could have been as bad as the sight of Wolf Creek once the smoke started to clear and men battled to douse the flames of the burning buildings. Logan Munro had ministered to the wounded, including Marshal Sam Gardner, and pronounced Li Chang and Ann Haselton dead.

He also pronounced death on Fred Garvey, Slim Tabner, Jeremiah Barnes, Hank Jones and Jed Stevens, along with four of the Danby gang.

Almost immediately, like human buzzards, Wil Marsh—with some help from Elijah Gravely the undertaker—started arranging the bodies of the gang into suitable poses. Then, with his tripod and camera, he methodically set about taking the photographs that he imagined he would be able to sell to the Eastern magazines.

Sheriff Satterlee took control and started to form a posse from the available able-bodied men and whoever had horses. He called an impromptu meeting in his office and prepared to swear in whoever could go.

"Doc Munro, you had best stay in town and look after the wounded," he said, as he looked over the volunteers gathered in the office.

"The hell with that, Sheriff. I have done what needs to be done. Doctor Cantrell knows enough medicine, as a dentist, to look after the wounded here. And Martha Pomeroy is a capable nurse." He started filling his meerschaum pipe. "I took the Hippocratic Oath and it is my duty to tend to the sick. I think I need to go, just in case any more of my friends here get hurt. And if we shoot any of that gang, it will be my solemn duty to treat and keep them alive."

He lit his pipe and his eyes narrowed as he blew out a stream of smoke. "Until we can hang the bastards, that is!"

CHAPTER THREE

By the time Bill reached Sheriff Satterlee's office, several men were already there, listening to Satterlee's plans on how best to catch the outlaws who had ravaged Wolf Creek. Among them were Jimmy Spotted Owl, town blacksmith Spike Sweeney, and two of Satterlee's deputies, Bill Zachary and Spence Pennycuff. Quint Croy, the town's other deputy marshal, was also there. Charley Blackfeather leaned against the back wall of the office. Next to him, to Bill's surprise, was Robert Gallagher, one of the clerks from Pratt's General Store. Gallagher was a young man of about twenty-three, who wore spectacles and, when not working, could usually be found with his nose buried in a book. Gallagher was extremely thin, and the heavy Smith and Wesson American in the holster on his right hip threatened to pull his gunbelt over his hips and down to his ankles at any moment.

Satterlee nodded to Bill when he entered. If the sheriff was surprised at the two Colts hanging from Bill's hips, and the third snuggled against his belly, he didn't show it.

"Bill, glad you got here so fast. We don't have time to mince words. Those sons of bitches did their best to make sure there wasn't a horse left in Wolf Creek. Lucky me and my deputies were down in Dogleg, so they missed ours. Got a couple of others too, along with a dead outlaw's mount, but we're still short. How many you got in your barn?"

"Half-dozen, plus Cholla. One of those is Fred Garvey's, so that one doesn't count."

"Fred won't be needin' his horse. He's dead, so you can add his bronc and yours to the number."

"There's another dead outlaw's horse in my barn," Bill answered. "As for my horse, I'm ridin' with you, Sheriff."

"You sure about that, Bill?"

"Nothing could stop me."

"Good. Head back to your barn and saddle up those horses. We'll be along in twenty minutes."

"I'll need a horse, Sheriff," Quint said. "Mine was one of those killed."

"We'll find you a mount," Satterlee assured him.

"Sheriff, you'd best leave the town deputy here," Charley Blackfeather spoke up. "In case you already forgot what I told you, that was the Danby outfit that hit us. Jim Danby likes to circle some of his men back after a raid, figurin' while a posse is out chasin' part of the gang the rest can finish what they started."

"Charley's right," Satterlee said. "Quint, you stay in town."

"But—" Croy started to object.

Satterlee cut him short. "No time for arguin'. Bill, get those horses ready."

"Right, Sheriff."

Bill opened the door and stepped outside, only to be greeted by a blood-curdling scream. Satterlee and the other possemen rushed out of the office.

"What the devil's goin' on?" Satterlee demanded.

Bill was standing stock-still. A plump, middle-aged matron blocked his way. Her dark eyes were wide with indignation, and her finger shook as she pointed at the hostler's bare upper torso, which was smeared with Jed's and Rojo's blood. She jabbed her parasol into Bill's chest.

"Sheriff, this man has no shirt on!" she exclaimed. "I demand you do something about it. It's indecent. Arrest him at once!"

Bill hadn't had the chance to pull his shirt on before the outlaws attacked. Now, in his haste to answer the sheriff's summons, combined with the shock of Jed's and Ann's deaths, Bill hadn't even realized he'd never fully redressed.

"Mrs. Pettigrew," Satterlee said, exasperated. "After all this town has just been through, do you really think I'm concerned about whether or not a man has a shirt on? Why don't you make yourself useful and try to help with the wounded, or else just go home?"

Edith Pettigrew was the widow of Seth Pettigrew, one of the founders of Wolf Creek, and considered herself, and her group of sewing circle ladies, the moral compass of the settlement. She was constantly badgering the marshal and sheriff about some perceived iniquity. The fact she was addicted to opium from Tsu Chiao's Red Chamber did not seem, to her, the least bit hypocritical—somehow it seemed only to heighten her moral indignation. She never went to the Red Chamber herself, of course. People would talk. She usually sent Dickie Dildine or Rupe Tingley to fetch her "medicine".

"George Washington Satterlee, I'll have your badge," she shrieked.

"Fine, Mrs. Pettigrew. You can have it once I've finished my business with the Danby gang. Now, just go home, or by God, I'll have you hogtied and carried there."

"You wouldn't dare!"

"Just try me," Satterlee snapped. "Bill, get goin'."

Mrs. Pettigrew scurried away. Satterlee sensed the shock in some of the posse members at his brusque treatment of a lady, even one as exasperating as her, and silently swore at himself. This kind of stress tended to bring out the rough edges of his past life, not a desirable trait in a public official—and not a side of himself that George Washington Satterlee wanted to show. But there was nothing to be done about it now, and no time to worry about it further. The Danby Gang had violated his town, and they were going to pay.

****

Twenty minutes later, fourteen men were assembled in front of Bill's stable. Joining the ones from Satterlee's office were three more cowboys, Billy Below, Joe Montgomery, and Phil Salem. Red Myers, one of the assistants from the tannery, was also present, along with Doctor Logan Munro, who carried his medical bag. Rounding out the posse was Derrick McCain, who nodded silent agreement as Montgomery loudly voiced his objections to some of the members.

"Sheriff, I thought I was joinin' a posse, not a Sunday school picnic," Montgomery complained. "We need the toughest hombres we can find to take on Jim Danby and his bunch, not a bunch of lily-livered, yella-bellied women."

"Joe, where the hell do you think I'm gonna find more men?" Satterlee questioned. "Fred Garvey's dead, Sam Gardner's shot up bad, and I've got to leave some people behind in case Danby decides to come back and hit the town again. Spike, here, offered to stay back, but a lot of the folks in town don't trust him. Besides, I need his gun."

"Yeah, but Sheriff, look at what you've got. A half-breed Cherokee, who'd rather strum his guitar or play his harmonica than work; then there's Gallagher, a four-eyed store clerk who probably can't even see to aim a gun, let alone set a horse; and finally, Torrance, who no one ever saw with so much as a pea-shooter until this mornin'. Hell, none of 'em will do us any good out there, 'specially the livery man."

Satterlee gazed at Bill, who had thrown on his shirt, but had yet to button it. He took in the bullet scar on Bill's chest, and the old saber slash across his belly, both still coated with Jed's and Rojo's blood. He also hadn't failed to notice the Model 1866 Winchester Yellowboy repeater Bill slid into his saddle scabbard.

"Joe, I think Torrance might just surprise all of us. He's ridin'."

"Ridin' what? He don't even have a decent horse," Montgomery objected. "That fancy calico pony of his'll never keep up. Hell, it ain't nothin' but a spoiled pie-biter, everybody knows that. Horse like that is only fit for women or squaws."

Bill had said nothing, until now. He stalked up to Joe, and sank his left fist deep into Montgomery's belly. The young man doubled up, wrapped his arms around his middle, and collapsed to the dirt. He lay on his side, gasping for breath, eyes watering with pain.

"Montgomery, you can say whatever you'd like about me, but talk about my horse like that again and I'll kill you where you stand," Bill warned.

Whatever Joe intended to reply was cut off by Satterlee's brusque order.

"That's plenty out of both of you. We've got a big enough problem facin' us as it is, without fightin' amongst ourselves. Joe, soon as you get your air back, get on your horse and catch up to us. Bill, you hold your temper. Rest of you, get mounted. Every minute we stand around is another minute between us and the Danby bunch."

****

Bill's thoughts raced faster than the powerful horse galloping underneath him as the posse raced hell-bent for leather across the rolling Kansas plains. When he'd left Texas, he'd vowed to never again wear a badge or touch a weapon. Yet, despite that vow, here he was deputized, and in pursuit of one of the most vicious outlaw gangs plaguing the southern Plains.

As one of the considerable minority of Texans who opposed secession from the Union at the start of the War, Bill had refused to join the Confederate army. As far as he, and a lot of others, were concerned, the war had been started to support a bunch of wealthy plantation owners in the South and rich Yankees in the North. He'd never bought the argument advanced by many Southerners that the whole reason for secession was states' rights. Bill's opinion was that claim was so much horse manure. If the plantation owners hadn't wanted to keep their free labor, the war would never have been fought.

However, while Bill held no truck with the Confederacy, he was still loyal to Texas. Once the Comanches realized much of the male population of the state had gone off to fight, they intensified their raiding, hoping to take back some of the land they'd lost. When volunteer companies of Texas Rangers were once again organized, Bill answered the call. Before long, he rose to the rank of sergeant.

By the time the war neared its end, the Rangers found themselves dealing with white renegades as much as Indians. Deserters from both armies, mainly the South, and outlaws in general flocked to Texas. The wide-open spaces and lack of law provided plenty of opportunity, and places to disappear. The people of Texas soon found out many of those white renegades were far more trouble than any Comanches.

It was during a confrontation with one of those bands of deserters when Bill had his first encounter with Wes Hammond. He and five men from his Ranger company had been searching for the band which included Hammond for several weeks. They finally caught up to them at a trading post some miles west of Bandera, where they'd already killed the proprietor and his family and were looting the place. When the Rangers arrived, the outlaws holed up inside the building. A two-hour gun battle ensued, during which one of Bill's men was killed, and another badly wounded. The standoff finally ended when a Ranger was able to get close enough to the trading post to set it on fire. Forced to flee the structure or burn to death, the outlaws raced into a hail of lead, which cut down all but one. Wes Hammond managed to escape being hit, and made it to his horse. Bill caught up to Hammond just as he was climbing into the saddle. He ordered Hammond to surrender, but Hammond whirled, saber in hand, and slashed Bill across the belly. Bill staggered back, and managed to fire one shot before Hammond could strike again. His bullet took Hammond in the upper right arm, causing him to drop the saber. Bill collapsed, while Hammond, leaving him for dead, pulled himself onto his horse and disappeared through the smoke and haze. Bill survived, but took several weeks to recuperate. Months later, he heard Hammond had left Texas and joined back up with his old guerrilla outfit, led by a man named Jim Danby.

After the war's end, with the Rangers effectively disbanded and replaced by the despised State Police, Bill took the town marshal's job in Blanco. He liked law work, and the citizens of Blanco, for the most part, liked Bill. He envisioned remaining as Blanco's marshal indefinitely, until the day Harold Perdue came home to find his wife, Georgia, in bed with Pete Channing. Harold was the mayor of Blanco, while Pete just happened to be Bill's closest friend. Instead of doing the sensible thing, leaving town fast, Pete shot Perdue dead in his own bedroom. Later, when Bill attempted to arrest him, Pete pulled his gun. Bill hesitated, not wanting to shoot his best friend. That moment of indecision nearly cost him his life when Pete put a bullet in his chest. Bill's two return shots tore through Pete's belly. The gut-shot cowboy lingered for three agonizing days before he died. After Pete's funeral, Bill turned in his badge, took off his guns, and left Blanco without looking back.

"So here we are again Cholla, chasin' outlaws," Bill murmured to his horse. "Reckon I don't need to ask how you feel about that."

Cholla merely twitched his ears and increased his

pace. True to his mustang ancestry, the big paint loved to run, and enjoyed nothing more than the thrill of the chase.

****

Little more than three miles outside of town, Satterlee ordered the posse to a halt. Lying on a creek bank were the bullet-riddled bodies of two young boys, each no more than nine years old. One still clutched a fishing pole.

"Those bastards!" Satterlee exclaimed. "That's Jody and Jesse Haskins. Just a coupla kids. No reason for Danby to do that."

"You reckon we'd better check the Haskins' place?" Spence Pennycuff asked. "Tracks're headin' that way."

"Yeah. Can't take the time to care for these boys properly. One of you toss a blanket over 'em, then let's keep movin',' Satterlee ordered.

"Sheriff, I don't reckon we'll find much left at Haskins' house," Derrick said. He indicated a thin wisp of smoke, barely visible against the hazy sky.

"Even more reason to swing by there," Satterlee answered. "Won't take but a minute or two. Let's go."

"Hold on, Sheriff. Someone's comin'. Appears to be Mack Haskins," Charley said, when a rider on a hard driven horse topped a small rise. He held a rifle, which he waved over his head. He pulled his horse to a halt once he reached the posse. A deep bullet crease, still oozing blood, marred his forehead.

"Sheriff," he called. "I was just headed into town. Bunch of riders hit my place, shot me and left me for dead, then burned the house down and ran off my stock, except Rowdy here. Mary's missing. Those men must've taken her. Got to locate my boys, make sure they're safe, then go after my wife."

"Slow down, Mack," Satterlee advised. "Same bunch invaded town, looted the place and robbed the bank. We're on their trail. Far as your boys, I'm sorry."

"What do you mean, Sheriff?"

"There's no easy way to break this. Your boys are dead, Mack. Shot by those men. They're right behind us, on the creek bank."

"Lord, no!"

Haskins buried his head in his hands, sobbing.

"Jimmy, you stay here with Mack," Satterlee ordered. "Help him get his boys home, then catch up with us if you can."

"We'll catch up with you all right," Haskins said. "Rowdy is fresh." He glanced at the young Cherokee cowboy. "Let's go," he barked, "I'm gonna lay my boys out in the house and kiss 'em, and then I'm ridin' with you to get my Mary back!"

****

Danby's gang had ridden west out of Wolf Creek for two miles, then turned due south, heading for Indian Territory. After pursuing them for three hours, Satterlee called for a twenty-minute rest break.

"What're we stoppin' for, Sheriff?" Red Myers demanded. "You can be sure Danby ain't."

"Won't do us any good to ride these horses into the ground," Satterlee explained. "Danby's mounts can't be in much better shape. Mack says they didn't get more'n two fresh horses from him, so they'll have to rest their horses, too."

"Unless they stole more further down the line," Spike Sweeney pointed out.

"In which case, it won't matter anyway," Bill said. "If they get fresh horses, they'll make the Nations long before we catch up with 'em."

"Torrance, if you're so worried about that spotted cayuse of yours, why don't you just turn back?" Joe Montgomery asked.

"I ain't worried about Cholla. He's got plenty of miles left in him," Bill replied. "However, most of the others don't. Like G.W. says, we rest 'em, or we lose 'em—and if we lose these horses, we lose Danby's bunch."

"Much as I hate to agree with Torrance, he's right," Derrick added. "Twenty minutes won't make much difference one way or the other."

Bill allowed Cholla a short drink from his canteen. While his horse then grazed, Bill studied the other posse members. If pressed, he would have had to agree with Montgomery's objections to some of the men chosen, starting with himself. Of course, no one in Wolf Creek knew of his background. Likewise, Rob Gallagher, and, to a lesser degree, Jimmy Spotted Owl, seemed unsuited to tangling with a gang of hardened outlaws. The same could be said for Doctor Munro. Bill knew the doctor had seen the results of combat as a surgeon, but was unsure as to his actual battlefield experience. At least there were no questions about Satterlee himself, nor either of his deputies. All were tough, experienced lawmen.

Red Myers, the tannery worker, and Spike Sweeney, the blacksmith, were riding side by side—two men who could be counted on in a fight. The four cowboys, Jimmy, Joe Montgomery, Phil Salem, and little Billy Below were grouped alongside their horses. Derrick and Charley were off by themselves, whatever thoughts they had locked in their heads.

All too soon, the twenty minutes passed, and the possemen were back in their saddles, galloping south once again.

****

Charley Blackfeather pulled his bay gelding alongside Bill and Cholla. The posse's pace had settled to a steady lope, a gait that would cover plenty of ground, but still conserve the horses as much as possible.

"Bill," he said, just loudly enough so only the hostler could catch his words, "I've been studyin' on you since we left town. Seems to me you know a bit more about this whole business than you're lettin' on. Want to share somethin'?"

"Just a gut feelin'," Bill answered. "Appears to me these tracks are a bit too plain, even for a bunch as big as Danby's."

"You think we're bein' led into a drygulchin'?"

"I wouldn't bet against it, would you? Besides, you're the one who said Danby likes to circle men back."

"That's right, I did," Charley agreed. "I still get the feelin' you know more about Danby than you're willin' to admit."

"Only know what I've heard," Bill said. "For now, let's just keep our eyes and ears open—and hope G. W. isn't so hell-bent on catchin' up to Danby he leads us straight into a trap."

"Right." Charley slowed his horse, to drop slightly behind Bill.

By mid-afternoon, the posse had reached a stretch of rougher terrain, land crossed by shallow ravines and dry creek bottoms. A creek bed, deeper than the rest and marked by stunted cottonwoods and scrub brush, came into view. Bill studied it for a moment, then urged Cholla into a faster gait, pushing him into a dead run until he reached Satterlee. The sheriff and his deputies were still at the front of the posse.

"Sheriff," Bill called.

"What is it, Bill?"

"Don't like the looks of that creek bed ahead. Perfect spot for an ambush."

"Danby ain't gonna waste the time to pull a bushwhackin'," Satterlee objected. "He's in too much of a hurry to reach safety in the Nations."

"I'm not so sure about that, Sheriff," Bill protested.

"Torrance, you let me worry about how to handle this posse," Satterlee snapped. "If you don't like my way of doin' things, then you can head back to town."

"You're in charge, Sheriff," Bill answered, with a shrug. He slowed Cholla back to a lope, falling once again to the rear of the posse. Just as he did, a flock of startled crows, cawing in alarm, burst from the trees alongside the creek.

"Ambush!" Bill shouted. He peeled off from the posse as a barrage of gunfire burst from the brush.

CHAPTER FOUR

Both deputies were shot out of their saddles at the first volley. Spence Pennycuff was shot right through his badge, shards of metal from it driven deep into his chest, along with the lead slug. He toppled from his horse, rolled several times, then lay face-down and unmoving. Bill Zachary took a bullet in his side, and another in his leg. He landed in a shallow depression, just deep enough to shield him from more gunfire. The badly wounded deputy pulled himself along on his belly for several yards, then collapsed on his face.

Phil Salem, the stout young cowboy, only twenty-two, had his horse shot from under him. His leg broken when the horse crashed, Phil attempted to crawl to safety, leg dragging uselessly, but was shot to ribbons by a hail of lead, which slammed into his side and rolled him onto his back. Phil's eyes, wide-open in death, stared unblinking into the blazing sun.

Sheriff Satterlee, Billy Below, Spike Sweeney, Red Myers, Joe Montgomery, and Doctor Munro, as well as Mack Haskins, swerved their horses hard to the right, racing for the shelter of a low ridge. Reaching it, they quickly dismounted, removed rifles and spare ammunition from their horses, and, with slaps on the rumps, sent the mounts trotting away, hopefully out of rifle range. After what had transpired back in Wolf Creek, they had no illusions about Danby and his men not killing the animals. The horses would be their first targets, leaving their riders stranded and easy prey.

Doctor Munro attempted to climb the slope and reach the downed men, only to be pulled back by Sheriff Satterlee.

"Sheriff, I need to try and save those men," Munro protested.

"I can't let you do that, Doc," Satterlee answered. "You'd be cut down before you made ten yards. Like it or not, you're trapped here with the rest of us."

Bill, flattened low over his galloping horse, reached the safety of a deep, eroded gully. Close behind him were Charley Blackfeather, Jimmy Spotted Owl, Derrick McCain, and Robert Gallagher, the bespectacled clerk. They dismounted, grabbed rifles from saddleboots, and took up positions along the gully's wall, where they were relatively safe, yet had a clear view of their surroundings.

"Looks like the sheriff and a few others made that ridge over yonder," Rob Gallagher observed.

"Yeah, but they're pinned down," Charley answered. "Can't move beyond either side of that rise, or stick their heads up without gettin' 'em blown off."

As if in answer to Charley's statement, Red Myers rose from behind the ridge, and started to point his rifle in the direction of the outlaws. Immediately, his head exploded in a spray of blood and brain matter, when a rifle slug punched through his forehead and ripped away the back of his skull.

"Well, hell," Charley said.

"Sharpshooter in that cottonwood over there," Bill noted. "Got to get him before he picks off all those boys."

He lifted his Winchester to his shoulder, aimed, and fired. A yelp of pain issued from the trees, followed by the rustling of leaves and cracking of branches as the sniper plunged to the ground, Bill's bullet through his heart.

"Took care of one, anyway," Bill muttered. The others looked at him in disbelief.

"Thought you'd never handled a gun, Torrance," Derrick said. "For a man who supposedly wouldn't touch a weapon, that was some shot."

"Had a little practice in the past," Bill answered. "Now, all we've gotta do is figure out how to get out of this gully, and get the rest of those renegades without gettin' ourselves shot to pieces."

"Seems to me we're in a bad way, with Danby and his men havin' all the advantage," Jimmy said. "They can move out of that brush and ride off anytime they like, but if we try and leave this oversized ditch they'll drill us all, easy. Well, if we're gonna die anyway, I'm gonna die shootin'. With any luck at all, I'll take a few of those bastards with me."

"Don't be givin' up quite yet, Jimmy," Bill adviscd. "Give me a minute or two to look around. There might be a way out of this fix."

"Don't see how," Robert Gallagher retorted. He was braced against the sandy bank, holding his .44 Smith and Wesson American revolver. He thumbed back its hammer and pulled the trigger. One of Danby's men stumbled out of the scrub, doubled over, his hands pressed to his gut. He staggered for several feet, then spun to the dirt. He lay moaning in pain.

"Gallagher?" Charley exclaimed.

"Saw that hombre slippin' through the brush, tryin' to

sneak up on us, so I plugged him," Gallagher answered, matter-of-factly.

"Yeah, but you nailed dead center him from this distance—with a *six-gun*."

Robert shrugged.

"Like Bill, I've practiced some, too."

"I reckon," Charley said. "Bill, you really think we can shoot our way out of here?"

"I think there's a chance, yeah," Bill answered. "This gully runs down to the creek where those men are holed up. I figure I can use it to reach the creek, then cross it and get behind 'em. That should catch them by surprise. When I start shootin' at their backs, it'll give you fellers a chance to get outta this spot, mebbe gun down a few of those hombres. With luck, Satterlee will figure out what I'm up to, and he'll make a break for it too. I'll just need you to draw their fire until I make it across the creek."

"Torrance, that's plain suicide," Derrick objected. "You'll be cut down before you get halfway across."

"Mebbe, mebbe not," Bill answered. "I only need a few minutes."

"There's gotta be another way," Jimmy said. "Why don't you—"

He was interrupted by a shout coming from the ridge sheltering Satterlee and the others.

"You men out there," Mack Haskins screamed. "You the ones who shot my boys, and took my wife?"

There was a moment of silence, then a shouted response.

"Yeah, I reckon we did. Surprised you lived long enough to follow us."

"You got my Mary there, send her back!"

"Sorry, can't do that. We've got plans for her. Don't

worry about her bein' killed, though. Once we're done with her, she'll make a fine squaw for some Indian buck."

"You stinkin', murderin' sons of bitches!"

Satterlee lunged for Haskins, too late, as the infuriated, crazed rancher ran up the ridge and into the open.

"I'll kill every one of—"

At least fifteen bullets tore into Haskins, slamming him backward. His body lay quivering, his blood soaking into the parched earth.

"They got another one of us," Gallagher said.

"And they'll get all of us if we just sit here waitin'," Bill answered. "Unless one of you can come up with a better plan, I'm headed across that creek. Appreciate your coverin' me."

"Torrance, listen to me for just one minute," Derrick urged. "See that side branch over there?"

"Yeah. What of it? It don't lead anywhere."

"No, it doesn't," Derrick conceded. "But I can ride along inside it while you head for the crick, and lay down better coverin' fire than just standin' here. Maybe with their attention on me and the rest of us, you'll get clean across without bein' spotted."

"That makes sense, Bill," Charley agreed. "I say let Derrick give it a try. Rest of us'll cover you both from here."

"All right," Bill answered. "Sure wish there was a way we could take a prisoner or two, though. That'd give us the chance to question 'em, mebbe find out exactly where Danby holes up in the Territories. I'd be willin' to bet my hat that's not his entire bunch we're facin'. I'm certain he left part of his men here to drygulch us, while he and the rest kept on ridin' south."

"I don't think any of us would take that bet, Bill," Jimmy said.

"No, we sure wouldn't," Charley confirmed. "Far as takin' prisoners, you leave that to me. Jimmy, Robert, you two think you can cover Bill and Derrick without my help?"

"We'll manage," Jimmy assured him.

"Then, Bill, it seems we're all set," Charley said. "I'm gonna slide on outta here."

"Just one thing first", Bill answered. He pulled Jed's Navy Colt from his waistband. "I need some spare ammunition for this gun. It's only got two rounds left."

"Gimme that gun," Charley said. "I'll load it while you get your horse."

"Much obliged," Bill said, passing the Colt to Charley. He headed to where Cholla stood, patiently waiting. The horse nickered when Bill approached, then nuzzled his cheek. Bill placed a hand on each side of Cholla's muzzle, then gently shook the big paint's head.

"Just like old times, eh, Cholla?" he murmured. Cholla snorted, and tossed his head. Bill placed his head against Cholla's forehead, then his nose to Cholla's right nostril. Man and horse stood, exchanging breaths, each absorbing the other's strength and spirit.

"Bill, I hate to interrupt, but if you're through makin' love to that horse, we'd better get started," Charley said, with a grin. "Here's Jed's gun."

Behind him, Derrick was already mounted, rifle lying across the pommel of his saddle.

"All right, and thanks. Sure hope Satterlee's clever enough to figure out what we're tryin'. Good luck to all of you," Bill said. He tucked Jed's gun into his waistband.

"You're the one who's gonna need it," Jimmy answered.

"Give me just one minute before you start," Charley ordered. He slipped silently into the underbrush and disappeared. Bill waited until a minute had passed, then heeled Cholla into a dead run. Derrick followed, reining his horse into the side gully. The minute he did, he opened fire in the direction of the outlaws. Behind him, Gallagher and Jimmy did the same.

Joe Montgomery spotted Bill as he rode for the creek bed.

"Sheriff, I told you not to bring Torrance along. The son of a bitch is runnin' out on us. I'll stop that bastard!"

"Joe, you fool, no! Looks like he's tryin' to draw those renegades' bullets," Satterlee yelled, uselessly. Montgomery leapt to his feet and leveled his rifle at Bill's back. Before he could pull the trigger, concentrated fire from the outlaws tore into him, dropping him in his tracks.

As Bill had hoped, Danby's men, distracted by the gunfire from the gully, didn't notice him until he splashed across the creek and circled behind them. Cholla's reins were wrapped around the saddle horn, Bill guiding the paint with knee pressure. He held a Colt in each hand, and began blasting away at the outlaws' backs as soon as they were in sight. Three of Danby's men died before any of them realized one of the posse had gotten behind them.

"Get that bastard!" someone yelled. Several of the renegades turned to concentrate their fire on Bill, but he was an elusive target. Cholla, experienced in battle, twisted and turned—taking a zigzag path and making himself and his rider almost impossible to hit. Bill put bullets into two more men's chests, another into one's belly. He grunted when a bullet clipped the top of his shoulder, and Cholla squealed with pain when one grazed his hip. Bill shoved his now-empty Colts into their holsters, pulled out his Winchester, and urged Cholla onward.

Derrick, reaching the steep end of the side gully, spurred his horse up the slope. The animal struggled, nearly going to his knees, but Derrick's strong pull on the reins kept him upright until they burst over the gully's rim. Derrick charged straight into the brush, adding his fire to that of Bill. He shot one man, then ran his horse right over another, trampling him.

"We can't just stay here and let Bill try'n handle this by himself," Rob Gallagher shouted, when he heard Bill's first shots. "Let's give him a hand, Jimmy."

Crouched low, he and Jimmy left the protection of the gully, running across the open plain, guns blazing. Jimmy shot one outlaw through the throat, then a bullet ripped through his thigh. He dropped to one knee, then rolled behind the scant protection of a large clump of prickly pear. He flattened himself behind the cactus, reloaded, and resumed firing. Rob, his gun empty, dove into an old buffalo wallow, gasping for breath. A moment later he also had reloaded, and reentered the fray.

"Men, Torrance has given us the chance we needed. Get mounted. We're goin' after those bastards," Satterlee ordered. He grabbed his horse's reins and swung into the saddle, not waiting for the others to follow. He galloped the mount over the ridge and straight at the outlaws, gun blazing. His gunfire was quickly joined by that of the other possemen.

Caught between gunfire from three directions, what Danby had thought would be a deadly trap for his pursuers soon turned into a rout for his men instead. Within the span of ten minutes, almost all of the drygulchers were dead or mortally wounded.

Bill spotted Wes Hammond as Danby's second-in-command climbed onto his horse, attempting to flee. He pulled Jed's gun from his waistband.

"Hammond!" he shouted. "Hold it right there!"

Hammond whirled his horse to face Bill.

"Tolliver! Thought I killed you back in Texas. How many lives you got, you son of a bitch?"

He pulled the trigger of his gun a split-second before Bill. Hammond's slug slammed into Bill's stomach. Fighting to stay in the saddle, Bill shot twice, both slugs from Jed's gun hitting Hammond in the belly. Hammond slumped over his horse's neck, then fell to the dirt. Bill pressed a hand to his middle, jackknifed, and slid off Cholla's back. He staggered up to Hammond, kicked the gun out of his hand, stumbled back to Cholla, and collapsed.

****

Derrick McCain was the one who found Bill. He spotted Cholla, who was standing over his rider, occasionally nuzzling Bill's face. Derrick spoke soothingly to the horse as he approached.

"Easy, horse. It's all right, bud. I'm gonna check on your friend, okay?"

Cholla snorted, and backed away.

"Torrance?" Derrick asked. "You still—"

Bill's eyes flickered open.

"Yeah, I'm still here. So far, anyway. Don't reckon for long, though."

"You just wait until I get the doc before you decide that, y' hear?" Derrick answered.

"All right," Bill said. "Check Hammond first, however. Make sure he's done for."

"You got Wes Hammond?"

"Right over there."

"I'll see to him. Be right back."

Derrick walked to where Hammond lay, crimson spreading over his shirtfront. Hammond's breath came in gasping wheezes, the death rattle deep in his chest.

"Hammond," Derrick said.

"You're still alive too?" Hammond asked, in disbelief. "Can't—understand it. Well, at least I got—one of you bastards. Put a bullet in Tolliver's gut. He's not gonna cheat death—this time. Reckon he'll join me in Hell right—quick."

"Tolliver?" Derrick repeated. "You mean Torrance, don't you? Bill Torrance."

"Hell, mebbe that's the name he's usin' now, but his real name's Ben—Tolliver," Hammond answered. "He was a Texas Ranger, durin' the War. Later I heard—he became a town marshal, down in—Blanco."

"Torrance? You certain?"

"Certain as you're standin' there, watchin' me die," Hammond answered. "You want proof? I sliced Tolliver's belly open with a saber when—he and some other Rangers came on us. He still managed to put a bullet—in my shoulder. Couldn't finish him off, but figured he was dead—anyway. Could've knocked me over with—a feather when I spotted him standin' next to you back in—Wolf Creek. Knew you, didn't recognize Tolliver's face, but I sure knew it was him when I saw that scar—across his belly. I'm the one give it to him."

Hammond coughed, choking on the blood welling in his throat.

"Well, I'll be damned," Derrick muttered. "Torrance, a Texas Ranger. That explains a lot. Hammond—"

His last words to the outlaw were left unsaid. Hammond had breathed his last. Derrick headed back to Bill's side.

"Well?" Bill said.

"Hammond's dead," Derrick answered. "The others are too. Charley tried to take a prisoner or two, but they went down hard—I reckon they saw a big black Seminole with a hatchet and figured givin' up wasn't the wise choice."

"Danby?"

"Not here. Like you figured, he kept on ridin', along with most of his men. We'll start after 'em in the mornin'. Gonna spend the night here and lick our wounds."

Derrick paused before continuing.

"Torrance, gotta ask you somethin'. Before he died, Hammond claimed your real name is Tolliver, Ben Tolliver, and that you were a Texas Ranger. Any truth to that?"

"Guess there's no reason to lie—about that now. Always figured it would come out—sooner or later," Bill answered. "Yeah, my real name's—Tolliver."

"Knew you were more than you claimed when I saw how you handled yourself durin' that ambush," Derrick said. "You mind if I tell Satterlee about you?"

"Yeah, go ahead. He'll find out soon enough— anyway. Besides, like I said, I'm gut-shot, doubt I'll— pull through. Rather have my real name—on my tombstone."

"Don't put yourself in the ground yet," Derrick advised. "You're one tough hombre."

"McCain, help me up, will ya?"

"Are you loco, Torrance?"

"Just do what I ask, please? Gotta—check on my horse."

"All right."

Derrick slid his hands under Bill's shoulders and helped him to his feet. Bill stumbled over to Cholla. He took the horse's muzzle in his hands.

"You all right, pard?" he asked the horse. Cholla whinnied, his nostrils flaring in excitement and flecked with blood.

"Guess you're not hurt—too bad," Bill said. "Lemme just get some ointment—and clean out that bullet slash."

"I can handle that," Derrick offered.

"No offense, Derrick, but I'd rather patch up Cholla my ownself," Bill replied. He dug a tin of salve and piece of cloth from his saddlebags, then cleaned out and dressed the wound on Cholla's hip. Once that was finished, Bill attempted to pull himself into the saddle.

"Torrance, just what the hell do you think you're doin'?" Derrick demanded.

"Goin' after the rest—of the bastards who killed—Ann," Bill answered.

"You ain't goin' anywhere," Derrick ordered. "It's one thing to let you doctor a horse, but you sure as hell ain't ridin' him noplace. You're gonna wait right here while I fetch Doc Munro. Be back quick as I can."

"Reckon I don't have a choice," Bill conceded, when he swayed dizzily, and slumped against Cholla's side. "Better lie back down."

"Now you're talkin' sense," Derrick answered. "I'll

84

give you a hand."

Once Bill was again stretched out on his back, Derrick looked at him and grinned.

"Reckon we're all obliged to you. You did a good job here—Tex."

Bill managed a weak smile.

"So'd you—Reb."

****

Bill lay thinking while he awaited Derrick's return.

Reckon it's true what they say about everything comin' around eventually. I gut-shot Pete, my best friend, and swore I'd never take up a gun again. Move to Kansas, take a new name, and live in relative quiet, until Wes Hammond turns up in the same town where I settled. So, I forget everythin' I vowed, dig out my guns, and join a posse to go after Hammond. Now, just like Pete, I'm lyin' here with a bullet in my own belly. Man can't cheat fate, I guess.

Bill's morbid thoughts were interrupted by Derrick's return. Accompanying him were Doctor Munro and Sheriff Satterlee. Munro knelt at Bill's side and opened his bag.

"I'm sorry I didn't get here sooner, Bill, but I was tending to Deputy Zachary. He's been pretty severely wounded, not to downplay the seriousness of your injuries," Munro apologized.

"No need to apologize, or to worry—about me, Doc," Bill answered. "Doubt there's anythin' you can do for me."

"You let me be the judge of that," Munro ordered. He opened Bill's shirt, to reveal the oozing bullet hole in his stomach.

"See, Doc," Bill muttered. "I'm gut-shot. Done for."

"What did I just tell you, Torrance? Your wound is not quite as serious as you imagine. The bullet went into your stomach, but then out between two of your ribs. I'm going to do what I can here, then once we're back in Wolf Creek I'll be able to work on you more."

Munro reached into his bag and removed a brown bottle.

"Wait a minute, before you start," Bill requested. "Sheriff, how bad did—Danby's men hit us?"

"Not as bad as it could have been, thanks to your spottin' that ambush," Satterlee answered. "Reckon if I wasn't so thick-headed, and had listened to you, none of this would have happened."

"You've got no way of knowing that, Sheriff," Derrick said.

"He's right, Sheriff," Bill agreed.

"Appreciate that, but it still don't make things better," Satterlee replied. "We lost four men, five if you count Mack Haskins. Pennycuff, Salem, Myers, and Montgomery are dead. Zachary may not make it, and Spotted Owl took a slug through his leg, so he'll be laid up awhile. Billy Below took a bullet across his ribs. Few inches to the right and he'd have been Billy Six Feet Below."

"Sheriff, it hurts too much to laugh," Bill moaned.

"I guess," Satterlee conceded. "Anyway, Robert Gallagher really showed his salt. Lost his spectacles, but that didn't slow him down none. He waited until one of those renegades was right on top of him, then shoved his gun right into the bastard's belly and pulled the trigger. Blew that son of a bitch's guts clean out through his backbone. Reckon we all sold Gallagher short."

Satterlee didn't mention exactly how Joe Montgomery had died. He saw no point in that. He hesitated before bringing up his next question.

"Bill, Derrick here tells us Torrance ain't your real name. Says Wes Hammond claimed you're really an hombre name of Ben Tolliver, a former Texas Ranger and marshal. Says you and Hammond crossed paths before."

Bill sighed deeply.

"Like I told McCain, there's no point—denyin' it. Yeah, Tolliver's my real name, and I was a Ranger. That's where I ran into Hammond—the first time. He's the one who put this scar—across my belly. Always wondered whether we'd—meet up again."

"Why'd you quit law work? Seems like you're a natural for it,"

Satterlee pressed.

"That's a real long story, Sheriff," Bill began.

"No time for long stories," Munro interrupted. "Let me work on Bill, G.W., so I can get back to treat the less severely wounded."

He lifted the bottle and uncorked it.

"Bill, this is going to hurt like the devil," he warned. "However, with any luck, it will keep your wounds from festering until we reach town."

"Stop jawin' and just get at it, Doc," Bill urged.

"All right."

Munro poured a generous amount of the stinging liquid into the hole in Bill's stomach, allowing more to run over the exit wound in his side. Bill screamed at the burning, almost unbearable pain.

"I'm sorry I had to do that, but it was unavoidable,"

Munro apologized. "Now, I'm going to bandage your wounds, as tightly as possible to stanch the bleeding. Once I'm done, if you feel strong enough, keep one of your hands pressed to your stomach. That will also help slow the blood's flow."

By the time Munro finished, Bill had passed out.

"He dead, Doc?" Derrick asked.

"No, merely unconscious. That's just as well," Munro explained.

"You really think you can save Torrance, or I guess I should say *Tolliver*, Doc?" Satterlee questioned. "Rarely hear of a gut-shot man survivin'."

"On the contrary, Sheriff," Munro answered. "In my experience as a battlefield surgeon, I have seen more than one man, with abdominal injuries worse than Bill's, survive."

"You mean *Ben*, Doc," Derrick broke in.

Munro flashed a tired smile. "Yes, you're absolutely right, Derrick. I imagine we'll have to start using his correct name. Anyway, it will be a challenge; however, I dote on challenges, so I am confident I can save Ben's life. In fact, just this morning, Charley Blackfeather gave me some ingredients for a new potion he states is fine medicine for ulcers. I plan on trying his concoction on Ben, here. An ulcer is a hole, very similar to some bullet wounds."

Munro didn't reveal the "ingredients" Charley had provided were green frogs. Most white men scoffed at Indian or Chinese medicines, while he was willing to try almost any cure. Munro's travels had demonstrated to him the white race didn't hold a monopoly on effective medications.

"Doc, if you're finished here, we'd best get back to

the others," Satterlee ordered.

"Indeed. We'll just need to get Ben to our camp."

"You and the sheriff go ahead, Doc," Derrick said. "I'll take care of Ben."

"Are you certain?" Munro asked.

"Positive," Derrick assured him.

"All right. You know where we've set up camp," Satterlee said. "Meet us there."

Ben Tolliver never awakened when Derrick lifted him to Cholla's back and tied him in the saddle, nor when Derrick pulled him off his horse, laid him gently on the ground, and wrapped him in blankets. When he finally did regain consciousness, it was full dark. The sound of a harmonica drifted through the still air.

"Must be Jimmy Spotted Owl," the injured man mused. "Always did like the way he plays that mouth harp."

He didn't recognize the melody Jimmy was playing, a refrain so mournful it was almost a dirge. All he knew was that tune certainly fit the occasion. He fell back to sleep with the notes echoing through his fogged mind.

Wolf Creek: Bloody Trail

CHAPTER FIVE

Derrick McCain sat on a rock at the edge of their impromptu camp, rifle across his knees. The campfire was too far away to provide any warmth, but close enough for its flames to send flickers dancing among the shadows. Derrick focused all his attention on his ears, alert for any suspicious noise from the darkness that surrounded them. He heard soft breathing, and a few light snores, coming from his sleeping comrades—dark bundles burrowed beneath protective blankets. Sometimes one of the wounded would moan in pain. Five of those bundles made neither motion nor noise, and never would again.

He could not help but start when he suddenly realized that someone was sitting on the rock beside him. The man was no more than a shadow at first, but then the firelight revealed him to be the Seminole scout.

"Damn, Charley," Derrick said in a hoarse whisper. "I never heard you come up, you scared the hell out of me. Where'd you come from?"

"I been pokin' around some," Charley answered. "Tryin' to find somethin' to tie some blankets to and rig up a travois in case the doc needs one or two when he sets out in the mornin'. Torrance and that deputy was hurt pretty bad, might not can ride."

"Out there in the dark?"

Charley shrugged. "Too dark to track, and too dark for most in this outfit to ride. But not too dark for a Seminole to look around a mite."

"I guess not. What did you find?"

"This and that."

Derrick waited, thinking the scout would elaborate, but he did not. They sat for awhile in silence.

Charley Blackfeather could tell that the white man was uncomfortable. He'd have been a lot more than uncomfortable, Charley mused, if I had been an enemy intent on slipping into the camp. He'd be choking on his own blood, trying to breathe through a windpipe that had been sliced open. Charley had done just that to many a sentry, starting when he was a boy in Florida.

Derrick shifted his weight, nervous, almost like he could read Charley's thoughts. Charley did not move, he only stared into the darkness. After a couple of minutes, Derrick broke the silence.

"Gallagher handled himself well in that ambush. Surprised us all, didn't he? And Torrance—I don't reckon I ever even seen him with a gun before today."

"Yep," Charley said. This time Derrick thought he would say no more, but then the scout turned to look directly at him and continued. "Seems like our hostler been carryin' a secret."

"I reckon so."

Charley grunted. "I just been bringin' my pelts in to Wolf Creek for a few months. But I already figured out, most ever'body in that town is carryin' a secret of one kind or another."

Derrick nodded. "I guess that's how it is, out here on the frontier. Especially with all the folks that have moved into town since the railroad came. Probably not so much with the ones that've been here since it was first settled, though."

"I heard some folks talkin', back before the ambush," Charley said. "Talkin' low among their selves when we slowed down for a bit, probably didn't know I could hear 'em. Red Myers, it was, and them deputies."

"Talking about what?"

"About Danby's gang bein' Johnny Rebs, same as some in this posse. How they wasn't sure who to trust. Mostly they meant Spike Sweeney, seems like, but they mentioned you, too. Said you was brung up in their town, but when the war come, you rode off to join the Rebels."

Derrick sighed. "I've been back home for years. Seems like they'd let that go. I'm not some drifter that followed the railroad here. My folks helped found the town."

"But you was Secesh."

"My family was from the South—Tennessee, originally. My pa brought us here on account of 'popular sovereignty.' He used to go on about it all the time."

"Popular sovereignty," Charley repeated. "You mean votin' on slavery."

Derrick's discomfort had been fading, since his companion had started conversing with him instead of sitting in stoic silence. Now, it returned tenfold.

"Well, yeah," Derrick said. "A lot of people who came to Kansas in those days came because they were on one side of that argument or the other."

"And your pa was for slavery."

"Yeah."

Charley chuckled, and a genuine smile lit his face. "I was agin it," he said.

Derrick could not help chuckling as well—the smile put him at ease a little. "I reckon that makes sense," Derrick said.

"Uh-huh," Charley agreed. "My pa had strong feelin's about slavery, too. On account of he was born one, back in Georgia. But he run off, and made it to the swamps. The Seminoles took him in, like they did a lot of others. He got adopted, took a Seminole wife. I was born in the Everglades. I been a free man my whole life."

Charley chuckled again, but this one was tinged with bitterness.

"Well, almost my whole life," he continued. "Until the end of the last Seminole war. I was in John Horse's band, and we was slow to give up. We was lucky we didn't get put in one of them filthy prisons, like Osceola died in. Instead they marched us out west to Indian Territory. We didn't even have our own land there at first, we had to live in the Creek Nation. And a lot of us had broke off from the Creeks, way back yonder in the Red Stick War."

"Sounds like your people have seen a lot of wars," Derrick said.

Charley nodded. "They kinda blend together, after awhile. Life is war, I reckon, for a lot of us, anyways."

"I wish that when a war ended it would stay ended," Derrick said.

Charley stared at him again. "So you rode Secesh on account of your pa."

"More than anything, I reckon," Derrick said. "And my brothers. They both rode east and joined the Confederate Army. They told me to stay home and help out on the farm, that I was too young to fight—but I followed after them anyway, and I joined up too."

"But you came back," Charley said.

"Yeah, when the war was over I came back. My brothers died in Tennessee."

"Not when the war was over," Charley said, his voice suddenly cold. "When the war was still goin' on. You came back to this neck of the woods—or at least this side of the Mississippi."

Derrick stiffened, and his grip on the rifle tightened.

"For somebody that's been so quiet all day," Derrick said, "you sure have a lot to say all of a sudden."

"You think I been talkin' to pass the time?" Charley said. "I come over here to let you know."

"Know what?"

Charley produced his Bowie knife—seemingly from thin air—and waved it before Derrick's face.

"Loosen your holt on that rifle, son," Charley said. "Don't make no sudden motions."

Derrick reluctantly did as he was told, and Charley took the weapon away from him.

"Now, you just set there," Charley said. "I got some more talkin' to do."

"Let me know about what," Derrick repeated.

"Who *I* am, and who *you* are."

Charley set the rifle down and took the knife away from Derrick's face.

"I know you didn't spend the whole war back East," Charley said. "You was in Centralia, Missouri, in September of 1864 with Bloody Bill Anderson and a bunch of others that rode with Quantrill. Danby was there, too. And me. I was there."

Derrick shook his head slowly, closing his eyes briefly and sighing. Charley kept talking.

"I've seen you around town a time or two, comin' and

goin', but I never got a good look at you. Not till today, when Danby's bunch hit town. I seen him takin' shots at you and Torrance—I reckon it was seein' you and Danby together that done it. But I remembered. I won't never forget that day."

Charley pushed his face close to Derrick's. "Look close, boy. You remember me now?"

Derrick's eyes widened. "Damn," he said softly.

"I reckon we all look alike to you Rebs," Charley said. "But you stuck in my mind right off that day, on account of at first I thought you was a Cherokee. You favor one. I was wearin' this same hat, if that helps—though we was all wearin' blue on my side."

"No—I remember. I remember you now."

Derrick McCain put his head in his hands.

****

Charley Blackfeather had been reliving his memories all day. He had kept a close eye on Derrick McCain the whole time the posse was on the outlaws' trail, and hung on the snatches of conversation coming from Red, the tanner's helper, about McCain's past.

Charley figured he had more reason to distrust ex-Confederates than anyone else on the posse—and not just because of his black skin. In his youth, his people had fought the U.S. Army—not only to resist forcible removal from their homeland to an unknown country west of the Mississippi, but to resist demands that they turn over their black members to be sent into slavery. Osceola himself had a black wife—he and many other Seminoles were willing to risk their lives to keep their black brothers and sisters free.

The Black Seminoles had their own fighting bands, with leaders like John Horse and John Caesar. Charley accompanied his father to war when he was only twelve years old—and continued in that struggle when he was a man, long after his father had fallen. John Horse surrendered to the Army only after they had promised his band freedom if they agreed to accompany the other captured Seminoles to Indian Territory. Then came the long walk—countless Seminoles perished along the way.

Once in Indian Territory, the Seminoles were forced for many years to live in the Creek Nation. The Seminoles had broken away from the Creeks many years before—and after the Red Stick War ended in 1814, Seminole numbers had been swelled by traditionalist Creeks fleeing Alabama.

Many of their Creek neighbors in Indian Territory had slaves—as did many Cherokees, Choctaws and Chickasaws. Black Seminoles, many of whom had lived their whole lives as free warriors, became the frequent targets of slave-catchers who were as likely to be Indian as white. The unwary black Indian could find himself kidnapped and sold into slavery—sometimes even by the red Seminoles who had been their battle comrades. John Horse led a large group of Black Seminoles to Mexico, where there was no slavery, and offered their services to the Mexican army.

Charley Blackfeather had not gone with them. There were communities of free black Indians in the Creek Nation, and a large number of full blood Creeks and Seminoles who held onto the old ways and opposed slavery. Charley had cast his lot among them. Eventually, like his father before him, he took a full blood Seminole woman as his wife. Her name was Hachi, and she bore him three children, two sons and a daughter.

But life, it seemed to Charley, meant war—and peace was only the brief interlude between battles. War came once more to the Seminoles, and once more, slavery was a factor.

The United States was divided by a great Civil War. Both sides sought the Indian Nations as allies. The leaders of all five of the so-called "Five Civilized Tribes"—Cherokees, Creeks, Chickasaws, Choctaws, and Seminoles—allied with the Confederacy. Many of those leaders had established plantations along the Red and Arkansas Rivers, and owned slaves. But some citizens of those tribes—especially Seminoles and Creeks—opposed both slavery and the Confederacy.

Indian Territory, too, was divided by Civil War.

Feeling threatened by their pro-Confederate governments, thousands of pro-Union Indians flocked to the camp of the old Creek warrior Opothloyahola. With their women and children, they marched north toward Kansas, where the Union Army had promised to give them sanctuary. Charley and his family were among them.

It was not to be a peaceful exodus. Confederate forces—including Cherokee and Choctaw troops, as well as some Texas Rangers—attacked the emigrants. The journey to Kansas became a running battle. Of nine thousand Opothleyahola followers, two thousand died. Charley's sons, aged sixteen and fourteen, fought valiantly. The youngest, named Billy for his grandfather, fell at Round Mountain. The eldest, Jack, was killed at Chustenahlah.

They finally arrived in Kansas in December, and were sent to refugee camps near Fort Belmont. Most of the

Indians had only the clothes on their backs. The federal government was not prepared to accommodate so many people in winter, and did not have sufficient food or shelter. Many more of Opothleyahola's followers died of sickness and exposure. The old chief Opothleyahola was among those who perished. So was Charley Blackfeather's wife, Hachi, and their daughter, May.

Many of the surviving warriors were eager for revenge on the Confederates—the white and Indian ones alike. Union Indian regiments were formed—mostly Seminole and Creek, but with a good number of Cherokees and a handful from other tribes. Charley, like many escaped slaves and free blacks from the Indian Nations, joined a Kansas colored regiment. Most of its troops were ex-slaves from Missouri and Arkansas, but about a third were from the Nations, and most of that number were Seminoles.

Over the next three years, Charley saw action in Indian Territory, Arkansas, Kansas, and Missouri. On more than one occasion, his outfit fought against guerrilla bands—Charley came to view those Southern irregulars as the lowest of scum.

On September 27, 1864, that opinion was solidified forever.

Charley's company—what was left of it after a lengthy period of campaigning with no replacements—was attached to the 39th Missouri Mounted Infantry. The largest part of the Union force in the region had moved east to defend St. Louis—the 39th was charged with preventing guerrilla depredations along the Kansas-Missouri border.

They received word of just such a depredation—a bloody guerrilla raid in Centralia, Missouri. The 39th rushed to the town's rescue. Late in the afternoon they spotted a small band of Rebs, and the commanding major ordered a full-on charge at them. Charley and many other seasoned veterans were very uneasy about those tactics, but in the heat of the moment there was no time to argue. Major Johnston ordered his men to fire a volley into the fleeing guerrillas.

As soon as their weapons were discharged, the trap was sprung. The hills around them came alive with whooping Rebs, busting forth now from their hiding places. It was the oldest trick in the book, and the Yankees had blundered right into it.

Hundreds of Confederate raiders were upon them, and there was no time to reload. Most of the Rebs carried revolvers—in some cases, several of them. The firepower was withering, and the Yankees were scattered—it quickly turned in to a rout. The Missouri Union men and their black comrades rode desperately, trying to find an escape avenue, but there was none. Men and horses fell screaming all around Charley. Rebs rode down unsaddled Yankees—trampling some, shooting others, and occasionally slashing at them with sabers.

Charley saw his friend Sango Chedakis several yards away; the younger Seminole had been thrown from his dying horse and seemed dazed himself. He had lost his weapons in the fall. Sango's father, Cudjoe, had been one of Charley's oldest friends, since they had fought together as teens back in the Everglades. Only a couple of years older than Charley, Cudjoe had stepped in and taken him under his wing when Charley's father died in battle. Cudjoe and Charley had been taken prisoner and sent to Indian Territory together, and their sons played together. Cudjoe had been killed in the flight of

Opothleyahola, the same as Charley's two boys; in the years since then Charley had taken his dead friend's son under his own wing, and in some ways, they had become to one another the father and son each had lost at the hands of the Rebels.

Charley had barely had time to register Sango's plight when one of the Confederates galloped past the youth—a lanky, hatless man with a shock of red hair. A saber flashed in the sun, and Sango's head sailed away from his body in a bloody arc. The Rebel never slowed down. His face was burned into Charley's memory, though—and he saw it again, on the day Danby's gang raided Wolf Creek. Rebel Red wasn't among the bodies of the outlaws left behind with Wes Hammond to ambush the posse—which meant he was still out there, among the killers they were still pursuing.

Before Charley could react to Sango's death, his own mount was shot from under him and he was sent hurtling to the ground. He twisted and hit the grass in a roll, coming up with his Bowie knife and tomahawk both drawn. He surveyed the scene—and saw Union soldiers throwing down empty rifles and raising their hands in surrender, only to be executed. Some begged tearfully for their lives, to no avail. Raiders stooped over fallen Yankees and scalped them or cut off pieces of them for souvenirs.

Such sights no doubt instilled ever more fear into the Yankees who still fought on, but had little effect on Charley Blackfeather. In his world it had always been standard battlefield behavior. He had not only seen it before, he had dealt it out—and he had no illusions that any amount of begging would prevent him from suffering such treatment from an enemy, nor would it ever have occurred to him to try even if he thought it might.

A laughing Reb on a black horse charged straight at him. Charley jumped aside and hurled his tomahawk in a fluid motion. It thunked into the front of the man's skull, splitting his face like a melon. Charley leaped into the saddle even as the dying Reb slid to the ground. Charley took the reins and sped toward the opening of the draw.

Three men from his unit, still mounted, wheeled away from the slaughter and joined him in his flight. For one mad moment, Charley thought they might actually make it.

But then a group of Confederate horsemen cut them off and blocked their way. Within moments, more Rebs came from behind. They were surrounded.

"Hold up, boys," one of the Rebs called out to the others. He was a thin, hawk-faced man. His eyes were wild with bloodlust, and his mouth was twisted into a hateful sneer.

"Hold your fire!" the man commanded.

"But Captain Danby!" one of the men answered. "We got 'em!"

"Oh, we got 'em," Danby said. "We got ever' one of the sumbitches. But there ain't no need to be in a hurry now, we got this thing won."

Charley's gaze was drawn to a hatless young Reb who was reined in beside Danby. He was in his early twenties, with a shock of dark hair and dusky skin. He was an Indian, probably Cherokee.

"Ain't no need to rush," Danby was saying. "I mean, look at what we got here. We got us some live niggers in Yankee blue—been shootin' at white folks! A quick death is too good for 'em. We need to do somethin' special, make a good example."

"Like what, Jim?" one of the men said. He was tall and rangy, with long stringy hair.

Danby's sneer grew wider. "Well, Wes, I say we skin 'em alive." He gestured at the dark youth beside him. "You're pretty handy with that lasso, kid, and I seen you back at the train standin' around like you was lookin' for somethin' to do. Rope me that big buck yonder with the feathers, looks like he's most likely to give us trouble." He laughed. "Maybe we can braid you a new rope out of his hide!"

The youth hesitated. Danby stared at him, the sneer fading.

"I give you an order, boy," Danby said.

The lanky redhead who had killed Sango snickered. "The kid ain't got the guts for man's work," he said.

"Shut up, Davis," Danby said. "McCain'll do what I tell him, won't you, boy?"

"It's one thing to shoot 'em down," Derrick said. "Hell, they shoot ours when they catch 'em. But I don't want any part of torturing people like we was wild Injuns."

Danby leaned over in the saddle and back-handed the youth. "You little shit!" he said. "You'll do what I say! You'll skin them monkeys your own damn self, or by God, I'll skin *you*!"

"Like hell!" the young man said, and reached for his pistol.

There could be no better opportunity for Charley and his comrades. He charged directly into the distracted Rebs and burst through their line, the other three black soldiers behind him.

The Rebs gathered their wits quickly. A fusillade rained on the fleeing soldiers. Charley felt the bullets plow into him. One in his right shoulder, another breaking a rib in his back, a third in his left hip. He leaned close to the horse's neck and held on, as if he could outrace the bullets. He never looked back.

But he survived. He escaped. The other three did not. Charley spent the last months of the war healing. His dreams were haunted for some time by Danby and the young man with the Cherokee face.

And now fate had brought them back together. Some people would regard that as an incredible coincidence. Others would realize that it was not so incredible—that Kansas and Missouri comprised a world much smaller than one might expect, and that the war in those border states was a web whose strands connected everyone in one way or another. Truth to tell, there were probably several former Union Jayhawkers and Confederate border ruffians living in Wolf Creek, interacting every day, and that was only to be expected. This meeting, such people would say, was no different.

But Charley Blackfeather knew better. He knew that there was a symmetry to the spirit world, that led inevitably to balance. When he saw Danby and McCain on the streets of Wolf Creek, Charley knew that it was the drawstrings of nature pulling them all together. He had privately concluded that Wolf Creek was a mystical place, imbued with powerful medicine—a thin place between worlds, that drew lost souls to it with the suction of a whirlpool acting on driftwood.

Of course, he would never be able to explain his beliefs on the subject to white folks. He didn't have the words, and they didn't have the ears to hear.

But here he sat, beside a ghost from his past, and he knew it was so.

CHAPTER SIX

Derrick McCain lifted his head and sighed deeply.

"I used to worry every day that someone was gonna come into town and recognize me from those days. I guess, as the years went by, I just put it farther and farther back in my mind. And now, here you are." Derrick's eyes narrowed. "Why didn't you say something earlier, in front of everybody?"

Charley studied him a moment.

"On account of you got me puzzled," the scout finally said. "At first I thought maybe you was workin' with the outlaws—you did before—but now I ain't so sure. It was plain to me that Danby recognized you, same as I did, but seems like it come as a shock to him. And you wasn't play-actin' this evenin' at that ambush."

Derrick nodded sadly. "But I reckon it's just too much of a stretch. I don't guess you expected to find somebody who rode with Quantrill bustin' sod in Taylor County."

"Wasn't expectin' it, no," Charley said. "But wasn't surprised. Fact is, I think I've spotted one or two others. Not from the same band as you and Danby, but I know I've seen 'em before. I've got an eye for faces. I would've placed you, if'n I'd seen your face good before today."

105

"How come you ain't said nothing about them?"

Charley shrugged. "I ain't got no personal stake with them. I ain't tryin' to re-fight the whole war—around here, that would have no end."

Charley put the knife back in its sheath.

"You ain't gonna stab me?" Derrick said.

"Not sure. Not right at this moment, I don't reckon. Just didn't want you to panic. I remember that you saved my life that day, whether you meant to or not."

"It was a bloody day," Derrick said. "One of the bloodiest. And I was tired."

He looked away from the Seminole, into the darkness.

"I had never really planned on taking such a course," Derrick said. "I really did ride east to Tennessee, after my brothers, to join up. We were all there in the Army of the Mississippi, under General Albert Sidney Johnston. General Johnston died at Shiloh—and so did my brothers. A whole hell of a lot of people died at Shiloh, it was a mess."

Derrick closed his eyes for a moment, lost in a bad memory. "And it wasn't long after that when I got the news from Wolf Creek. Some Jayhawkers had rode out to my folks' farm one night and hung my pa from a barn rafter. Like I said, Pa was strong on popular sovereignty back in the 'fifties, and on the South. And on slavery—he always said slavery was an excuse Yankees tried to use to cripple the South in Congress. Anyways, he didn't make many friends in these parts. I always sort of guessed that he was doing more than talking back then—they called this Bleeding Kansas for a reason, after all. Pa had friends that was hacked up by John Brown and his sons."

Derrick spat. Charley noticed that his fists were now clenched at his sides.

"I was supposed to be here," Derrick said. "Helping him and Ma. Instead I was hundreds of miles away. Pretty soon, it got to the point that I didn't see any sense in lining up with thousands of other Southerners, face thousands of Yankees in a field, and then blowing the hell out of each other day after day. Not when the sons of bitches that murdered my pa was running scot free along the Kansas-Missouri border.

"So I quit my post and drifted back West. I found some old boys who felt the same way about Jayhawkers as I did, and didn't see the need to follow a lot of rules when dealing with them."

"Quantrill," Charley said.

"Yes, Quantrill. And all the hardcases that rode with him. There were several bands, and when they all come together we numbered in the thousands. There was Bloody Bill Anderson—his pa was murdered by Jayhawkers too, or so he said. And Frank James and his little brother Jesse—the Union bastards hung their old step-father from a tree and tortured him. And there was Cole Younger, Little Arch Clement, Clel Miller, and George Todd and there was Jim Danby and his lieutenant, Wes Hammond.

"We believed in hitting the Yankees hard. At first, I hated it and I loved it at the same time. I was doing things that the Good Book told me it was a terrible sin to do— but I was doing them to defend my homeland, and to avenge my pa. Every time I killed a Jayhawker up close, I imagined it was one of the men that hanged my father— and maybe some of them were.

"But it got out of hand…*way* out of hand. You know what happened in Lawrence. We pretty near burned that town to the ground. Four hundred of us rode in at dawn and unleashed holy hell on them—everybody knew that town was the base for all the Jayhawkers and Redlegs in the area. I hear we killed a hundred and fifty men out of the two hundred that lived there. I don't know. I wasn't counting. I just know that the screaming mothers and wives and children still wake me up nights."

Charley nodded, almost imperceptibly. He heard the screams sometimes, though for him, it was not so much a haunting as an echo.

"Things got pretty bad for us around Kansas after that," Derrick continued. "We had to light out for Texas for a spell. While we were gone, the Union Army declared martial law in Missouri. And they arrested a bunch of women for being guerrilla sympathizers—including Bloody Bill's sister. They put them in a stone jail, and it mysteriously collapsed in on itself and crushed those poor ladies to death.

"Bloody Bill wasn't just mad after that, he was plumb crazy. He started scalping people—and a bunch of the others did, too. They would tie Yankee scalps to their saddles, and they'd flap in the wind when they rode into battle. It was downright savage. It was like the last veil of righteousness had been lifted away and we had become no better than heathens, you can't imagine how terrible it was."

Derrick realized that Charley was staring at him curiously, with a bemused smile.

"Oh," Derrick said. "I meant no disrespect. It's just that—well, I saw the bodies of some Confederate Cherokees that had been captured by some Union ones. The bluebelly Cherokees cut those poor bastards into pieces and then burned what was left, the smell was awful."

Charley politely nodded his understanding, and Derrick continued his tale.

"It weighed on me more every day," Derrick said. "I started thinking about Hell. It was hard to imagine a worse place than where I was already at, but if there was one I was surely headed straight into its mouth, and I could get sent on my way there any day. I was just sick of it all. The hunger for vengeance just sort of petered out after awhile, I guess. Instead of thinking about my dead pa, I started thinking about my living ma and how ashamed of me she would be."

A look of disgust passed over Derrick's face.

"And then came Centralia," he said. "We hit the town that morning, just like Danby hit Wolf Creek today. And we tore up the railroad tracks—when the train rolled in we ordered everybody off of it and robbed them. There were about two dozen Union soldiers on that train, coming back from leave. Bloody Bill made them strip naked and stand in formation—and then the killing started."

Derrick shifted uncomfortably on the rock and then continued.

"I didn't join in. Danby did, he took some scalps and God knows what else—he gave me a real funny look when he saw me just standing off to the side.

"I thought I was going to puke. I feel like puking now. I used to admire Bloody Bill, see. I used to look up to him. We had a lot in common, and I wanted to be like him—a cold, hard avenger. But now, he was an animal, a demon from Satan's pit—and I didn't want to be like him anymore. But with all the things I done, I was scared that deep down, I already was like him. I'm still scared that I am."

Derrick's voice had gone thinner. He took a few moments to regain his composure.

"You know the rest," he said after awhile. "We knew you boys would come charging in to the rescue, so we laid a fine trap. I could deal with that, better than I could robbing old ladies on trains or murdering naked prisoners who was just on leave visiting their families. The ambush was war. And our side may have stopped taking prisoners—but so had the Yankees, and I'd had some good friends shot down in their tracks with their hands in the air. I didn't like it, but I had done it—on the field, in the heat of battle, but not in the cold blooded way Bloody Bill ordered it done on that train.

"But when Danby ordered me to—to help skin prisoners alive, I couldn't take any more. I snapped. Funny thing is, if he'd just ordered me to shoot you, out there on the battlefield, you'd be dead now."

"Danby didn't seem too happy with you that day, when you didn't obey him." Charley said. Despite the emotion emanating from Derrick like shimmering heat, Charley's voice was impassive.

"I reckon that would describe it," Derrick said. "After you got away, he ordered one of his men to shoot me. I took a bullet in the chest and they left me laying with the dead Yankees. My dear old friends took my boots and my duster, and most everything else, same as they did to most of the corpses. They took all their own dead and wounded with them, except for me. Some kind folks that lived close by found me and took me in till I could ride. It was a miracle I was alive.

"I borrowed a horse from them—I sent them money for it later—and made my way to the Cherokee Nation. My pa used to run a school there, before we moved to

Kansas—I still knew people who would take me in and keep me hid while I finished healing."

"So I was right," Charley said. "You did live in the Cherokee Nation."

"Just for awhile, when I was a little kid," Derrick said. "I'm not Cherokee. Pa just moved there for the job. My people are from Tennessee, like I said."

Charley smiled. "So are the Cherokee. I bet you got some Cherokee blood in you, way back yonder somewhere. You got a Cherokee face."

Derrick was beginning to tire of Charley's talk about his face. Others had made similar comments throughout his life—especially in Indian Territory—but somehow he found that the Black Seminole hammering at the subject was making him especially annoyed.

"Anyway," Derrick said, "now you know my story. I made my way home and tried to put all that behind me. Then the outlaws hit town, and I saw Danby. And I heard the screaming women—and that pitiful little Chinese child. And all the anger and shame came back to me. I felt like—I felt like maybe, if I could help bring them in, be on the side of the angels just this one time, then maybe somehow I could make up for all the bad I've done. Maybe the scales would be balanced for me."

Charley's head jerked around as if he'd been struck. *Balance.*

Charley Blackfeather understood the need to restore balance. It was the primary spiritual goal of his people, before some of them started taking on white man's ways.

He also understood violence. He thought back on the Florida plantations he had raided with John Horse, the soldiers he killed and fed to the alligators, the things he had done to white and Indian enemies alike in the Civil

War. He doubted McCain's "sins" could compare to his own actions. He did not consider them sins, though, and was not ashamed of them. It was the way of the world.

Charley understood a man fighting to protect his way of life, and he understood fighting for revenge. Most of all, he was struck by the parallels in their stories—there was some strong medicine there which should not be ignored.

"Well?" Derrick said. "Are you going to tell them about me?"

Charley stared impassively at the younger man for awhile.

"I won't say nothing," he finally replied. "I'll give you a chance to restore balance. Balance is the most important thing there is, to an Indian. To white folks, too, only most of 'em don't realize it."

Derrick nodded his appreciation, but then the Black Seminole continued.

"But I will have my eyes on you."

"That's fair enough," Derrick said.

"Sleep now," Charley said. "It's my watch."

CHAPTER SEVEN

G.W. Satterlee stretched, yawned, and then wearily scrubbed a hand over his face. He was getting too old for this. He had a comfortable bed in his house back in Wolf Creek, and yet he'd spent the night sleeping on the hard ground, just like in the days when he'd been hunting buffalo or scouting for the army.

But, at least he'd woken up this morning, he reminded himself. That was something four of the men who'd ridden out with him would never do again, and the same was true for a number of people back in the settlement. Not to mention Mack Haskins, the grief-stricken farmer.

The hour was well before dawn. A faint band of gray tinged the eastern horizon. A few yards away from the spot where Satterlee had spread his bedroll, Charley Blackfeather was poking the embers of the fire to life.

"I'll have some coffee boiling soon, Sheriff," the Seminole said.

"And I'll be more'n happy to drink some of it," Satterlee replied. "Obliged to you, Charley. Quiet night, wasn't it?"

"Real quiet," Blackfeather said. "Except for the wounded men moanin' now and again. But in war, that qualifies as quiet, I reckon."

"I didn't know we were at war," Satterlee said as he hunkered on his heels and held out his hands to warm them in the glow of the flames that had sprung up. It got chilly at night, out here on the plains. "I thought we were just chasin' down a band of murderin' outlaws."

"Same thing. It's all killin'."

Satterlee shrugged and said, "You may be right about that."

He straightened. A few more of the sleeping men were starting to stir. Satterlee walked over to where Dr. Logan Munro had propped himself up on an elbow.

"Mornin', Doc."

Munro pushed his blankets aside. He sat up and said, "I need to check on my patients."

Munro climbed to his feet. Like Satterlee, he moved with the creaky stiffness of a man who might not be old, but was certainly no longer young.

While Munro was making sure that Tolliver and Zachary had lived through the night, Satterlee walked around the camp, rousing the other men.

"Reckon there's a good chance Danby and the rest of his bunch made camp last night, so they shouldn't have gotten too much farther ahead of us," Satterlee said. "But they'll be pullin' out early this morning, so we'd better do that, too."

"What about the men we lost, Sheriff?" Rob Gallagher asked. "Are we going to bury them?"

"Not unless you've got a shovel tucked away in your back pocket, son. None of the rest of us brought one."

Derrick McCain said, "There's a little draw over yonder. Maybe we could put them in it and cave the bank down over them. It's better than nothing. Somebody could come out from town later and retrieve the bodies."

"That's not a job I'd want," Billy Below said.

"I could help with that," Sweeney put in. "Assuming I

make it back alive."

"So could I," Blackfeather added without looking up. He set the coffeepot at the edge of the flames. "We got another body, though, tucked behind that rise back yonder."

"Another outlaw?" Satterlee asked, and Charley shook his head.

"The farmer's wife," the Seminole answered. "I found her out a ways, when I was scoutin' up makin's for the travois. I reckon they was done with her, and didn't want her makin' noise or slowin' 'em down. So they throwed her away."

"Lord have mercy," Rob Gallagher said.

Charley grunted. "I reckon He was runnin' short on mercy yesterday. And so was they. I didn't bring her body on into camp because I didn't have nothin' to cover her with, and it didn't seem right. She's been shamed enough as it is."

Spike scowled. "So the whole time they was taunting Haskins, braggin' on what they was gonna do to her— they had already done it, and she was dead. Sons of bitches."

Satterlee nodded his agreement and then said, "All right, let's get to work while Charley's rustlin' up some grub. We can strip some clothes off these outlaw sons of bitches and cover the Haskins woman, then I reckon we can put her with her husband."

"Mary," Derrick McCain said. Everyone looked at him, so he explained, "He said her name was Mary."

It was a grim task, and covering up the bodies using only bare hands and knives to break off pieces of the gully's bank wasn't easy. By the time it was done, though, the smell of coffee hung in the early morning air, and that

115

made the men feel a little better.

"What about the outlaws we killed?" Gallagher asked.

"Reckon the wolves and the buzzards will take care of them just fine," Satterlee said. "We'll send their horses back to town, and replace some of the ones they slaughtered in the raid. How are the wounded men lookin', Doc?"

"Right now, I'm guardedly optimistic that Bill—I mean, Ben—and Deputy Zachary will make it. Their chances will improve greatly if I can get them back to Wolf Creek where I can care for them properly."

"What about me, Doc?" Jimmy Spotted Owl asked. A bandage was wrapped around his thigh where a bullet had ventilated it.

"It'll take more than a wound like that to kill you, Jimmy," Munro told him with a smile.

"Then I can go on ahead with the posse?"

"I didn't say that. You need proper medical care, as well."

"And I'm countin' on you to guide the doc and the other two back to Wolf Creek, Jimmy," Satterlee put in. "You know this area better than Doctor Munro does. Less chance of you gettin' lost."

"I'd rather go on with you, Sheriff, and tangle some more with those damn owlhoots," Jimmy said.

Satterlee shook his head.

"You're goin' back, and that's that." His tone, as well as his words, made it clear that there would be no argument.

The sun still wasn't up by the time the men had eaten breakfast, but the band of gray in the east had turned to a strip of red and gold, a colorful harbinger of the new day. Ben Tolliver and Deputy Bill Zachary were lifted onto the two crude travois Charley had rigged and tied in place. Dr. Munro would lead the horses pulling the badly wounded men, and Jimmy Spotted Owl would lead the string of outlaw mounts. There were no sentimental goodbyes. The four men simply started riding back to the north at a slow, steady pace so Tolliver and Zachary wouldn't be jolted around too much.

The other six surviving members of the posse mounted up, as well, and headed south toward Indian Territory.

Danby and the rest of those bloodthirsty butchers were up there ahead of them somewhere, Satterlee thought as he rocked easily in the saddle. Would the posse catch up to them today? Would any of them still be alive come sunset?

Hard to stay—but then, just getting up in the morning under the best of circumstances was always a gamble, wasn't it, Satterlee mused with a faint smile on his lean face.

****

"How many men do you reckon the gang still has left, Sheriff?" Billy Below asked while the posse was stopped to rest their horses, a couple of hours after sun-up.

"To answer that, I'd have to know how many of them there were to start with, Billy, and I don't," Satterlee replied.

"Maybe we've whittled 'em down to where we got 'em outnumbered."

"You can hope that if you want to, but I wouldn't count on it."

Robert Gallagher spoke up, saying, "If you consider

how many of them there had to be in order to spread out all over town like they did, and how many were killed in the raid and since then, there are probably about a dozen of them still alive."

Billy looked around at the other members of the posse, his lips moving a little as he counted.

"And six of us," he said. "That's two-to-one odds. How we gonna handle that, Sheriff?"

Before Satterlee could formulate a gruff reply, Billy Below smiled and said, "It's too bad you don't have that old Sharps of yours along, isn't it, Sheriff?"

"What good would that do?" Gallagher asked.

"The sheriff here used to be a buffalo hunter," Billy explained. "And like most of those fellas, he's a good shot with a long gun. I bet if we could get within a few hundred yards of the outlaws, Sheriff Satterlee could pick 'em off one at a time with his Sharps. I remember some cavalry troopers I was drinkin' with one time at the Wolf's Den tellin' me about when he used to scout for the army—"

"Don't go to tellin' tales," Satterlee growled. "We don't have the time for it. These horses have rested enough. Mount up."

Satterlee took the lead as the posse rode out. He felt the eyes of the other men on him. Some of them—the younger ones, anyway—were probably wondering about him. He wasn't necessarily ashamed of his past, but in his time as a politician, running for office as sheriff, he had learned to downplay certain of the more unsavory areas of it. It was fine to say that he'd served as a scout for the cavalry, but he'd just as soon not go into detail about some of the things he'd done during that time of his life.

Satterlee and Charley Blackfeather were both good

trackers, and Danby and the rest of the outlaws didn't seem to be taking any particular pains to cover up their trail. They followed the tracks without much difficulty. Satterlee knew they were counting on beating any pursuit to Indian Territory.

By midday, the posse hadn't come across any sign of the gang except the hoofprints they were following. Satterlee's keen eyes scanned the southern horizon for a dust cloud or anything else that would indicate they were closing in on their quarry. Frustration was growing stronger inside him.

He motioned Blackfeather up alongside him and said, "How much farther you think it is to Indian Territory, Charley?"

"If we make camp again tonight, we ought to reach there about the middle of the day tomorrow."

Satterlee frowned and lifted a hand to scratch his jaw.

"Danby's liable to be close enough by nightfall that he'll push on. If he doesn't stop and we do, we'll never catch him."

"If we keep ridin' after dark and he heads off in another direction, we're liable to lose the trail entirely," Blackfeather pointed out.

Satterlee sighed and shook his head. "You're not tellin' me anything I don't already know, Charley."

Quietly enough that the others couldn't hear, Blackfeather said, "We ain't gonna catch them before they reach the Nations anyways, Sheriff. I reckon you know that. What happens then?"

"Don't say that. I don't plan to turn back until I have to. Maybe we'll get lucky."

Blackfeather grunted. The sound was enough to make it clear he had his doubts about that.

A short time later, Satterlee stiffened and sat up straighter in the saddle. He had spotted a thin line of smoke rising into the blue sky up ahead. He pointed it out to the others and said, "Chimney smoke. Must be a ranch or some sodbuster's shack."

"Maybe we could get fresh horses there," Derrick McCain suggested.

"Not likely, but you never know." Satterlee pushed his horse to a slightly faster pace and called over his shoulder, "Come on."

If the place was a ranch, there might be horses they could swap for, as McCain had said, but if it was just a small farm, the sodbuster would be lucky to have a pair of mules. He ought to know whose spread this was, Satterlee thought. They were in Barber County now—despite being incorporated, the county seat of Medicine Lodge was little more than a wide place in the road, and their lawmen were part-time farmers who rarely let go of a plow. Even if it wasn't his own county, with no professional peace officers in the area he should at least be familiar with the settlements.

But, in fact, he probably hadn't been as diligent about such things as he should have been. If Spence were here, he would know. He made it his business to know everything, and that was what had made him such a good deputy.

Spence Pennycuff wasn't here, though. He was lying back there miles behind the posse in a gully, with a pile of dirt on top of him. The thought made a bitter taste rise in Satterlee's throat. He hadn't allowed himself to dwell on the death of his friend and chief deputy, concentrating instead on the job in front of him. He pushed the thought out of his head now. He could mourn for Spence later, after they were back in Wolf Creek.

The posse came in sight of a good-sized house built of lumber, which meant this was a fairly prosperous ranch they were approaching. Having lumber freighted out here wasn't cheap, and there sure as hell weren't enough trees on these Kansas plains to furnish that many boards. Satterlee narrowed his eyes and made out a sod barn and a couple of pole corrals beyond the house. You could find enough cottonwoods along the creeks to fashion a corral from the thicker branches, but that was about it.

The smoke rose from a chimney at one end of the ranch house. Billy Below said, "Looks like they got dinner on to cook. Maybe they'll share some grub with us. I could use a home-cooked meal."

Spike Sweeney, who seldom said anything, spoke up. "I think I know this place. The man who owns it brought in some horses to be shod, and he talked about it. Name was—" Sweeney paused and frowned in thought. "Mallory, Malachi, something like that."

"You think he'd have enough horses he'd be willin' to swap with us?" Satterlee asked.

Sweeney shook his head and said, "I couldn't tell you, Sheriff."

They were only a few hundred yards from the spread now. In the middle of the day like this, Satterlee expected to see folks moving around, going about their chores. Instead he didn't see any people or horses. The place looked deserted, which didn't bode well for them getting any fresh horses here. But they were this close; they would go on in anyway. Maybe get something to eat, like Billy said.

The first sign of life was a volley of echoing barks

from a couple of big yellow curs who came bounding out from behind the house. Dogs like that were a reassuringly commonplace sight around a ranch.

The area in front of the house was a welter of hoofprints, Satterlee saw, as the posse rode up. It was impossible to tell who had come and gone, or when. He reined to a halt, rested his hand on the butt of his gun, and called, "Hello, the house!"

Even as he called out, he looked at the windows, alert for any sign of movement, especially if it involved the barrel of a gun. They had ridden into one ambush; he didn't want to fall victim to another.

It was unlikely, though, that Danby would have stopped here, not when the outlaws were so close to safety in Indian Territory.

Charley Blackfeather moved his horse forward a little and said, "It don't look like anybody's here, Sheriff."

"But there's a fire in the fireplace," Billy said. "You can see the smoke."

Before Satterlee could respond to either of them, the front door opened and a man stepped out onto the small front porch. Instinctively, Satterlee's grip on his gun tightened for a second before he saw that the man was unarmed.

"Howdy," the man called. "What can I do for you fellas?" Something seemed to catch his eye, and he added, "Is that you, Sweeney?"

The blacksmith nodded. "That's right, Mister— Mallory, is it?"

The man smiled and said, "You've got a good memory. Yeah, it's Ezra Mallory. Are the whole bunch of you from Wolf Creek?"

"That's right," Satterlee said. "I'm Taylor County

Sheriff G.W. Satterlee. We're on the trail of a band of outlaws that hit Wolf Creek yesterday morning. They killed some of our folks and looted the town. Their tracks go right past your place here, Mallory."

"Good Lord!" the rancher exclaimed as his eyes widened. "I'm sure sorry to hear about the trouble befallin' the settlement, Sheriff. You're trying to chase down these desperadoes?"

"That's right. Are you sayin' you haven't seen them, Mr. Mallory?"

"I just got back a little while ago. My wife and I been over to a neighbor's place, about five miles east of here. We must've just missed those outlaws. A stroke of mighty good luck, if you ask me."

"Yeah," Satterlee said. Something about this situation didn't ring true to him, but he couldn't have said what it was other than a vague stirring of unease. "What were you doin' over at the neighbors?"

Mallory frowned. "I don't see as how that's really any of your business, Sheriff, but as it happens, the lady of the house was, uh, in the family way, and it was her time. My wife's helped out at birthin's before, so we went over there to see if she could lend a hand."

"How'd it go?" Satterlee asked in apparently idle curiosity.

"Fine, just fine. Mother and baby both doin' fine." Mallory seemed to be getting more nervous with each passing second.

"Glad to hear it. This county could always use another citizen." Satterlee changed tacks. "It'd be mighty helpful to us if we could swap some horses with you, Mallory. Might give us a better chance to catch those outlaws."

The rancher swallowed and shook his head.

"Sorry, Sheriff. I've got a couple of saddle mounts and some draft horses, but that's all. Not enough to do you any good. You're welcome to water your horses from my well, though."

Billy Below leaned forward in his saddle and said boldly, "We'd plumb admire to have a home-cooked meal, too."

"There's no time for that, Billy," Satterlee snapped. "Besides, Miz Mallory's probably tired out after that birthin' chore. She won't be wantin' any company."

"That's true, Sheriff," Mallory said. "I'm obliged to you for understanding."

Charley Blackfeather turned his horse and rode slowly to the left, so that he could see past the house and get a better look at the barn. At least, that's what Satterlee figured the scout was doing. He wouldn't have minded taking a look in that barn himself.

"What's that Injun doin'?" Mallory asked sharply.

"Oh, don't mind him," Satterlee said. "He's sort of simple-minded. He's half black, half Seminole. You know how those people are. Can't keep their minds on anything, and he's got it on both sides." He put a sharp note in his own voice as he went on, "Charley! You get back here now. Don't go wanderin' off."

"Sorry, Sheriff," Blackfeather said. "Jus' wanted to look at the pretty horses."

"Never mind the pretty horses," Satterlee said. He looked around at the others and pointed to the covered well. "Haul some water up and let your horses drink, and then we got to get back on the trail."

Gallagher, Sweeney, and McCain were all looking at him a little oddly. Billy Below was the only one who didn't seem to have noticed anything odd about the behavior of the sheriff and Charley Blackfeather over the past couple of minutes. He was still chagrined over the fact that he wasn't going to get a home-cooked meal out of the deal.

The posse members watered their horses while Mallory stood tensely on the porch, his hands gripping the railing. Satterlee took note of how white the rancher's knuckles were.

When they were finished at the well, Satterlee lifted a hand in farewell and called to Mallory, "Much obliged for the water."

"Good luck runnin' down those owlhoots," Mallory replied.

When they were out of earshot of the man, Satterlee said to Blackfeather, "How many horses did you see in the barn?"

"At least four," the scout replied. "Even if two of 'em belong to Mallory, that still leaves two extra. You reckon some of Danby's bunch was back there, inside the house?"

"I'd bet a hat on it. That's what had Mallory so spooked. They were probably in there with a gun on his wife. Might be some kids in there, too."

CHAPTER EIGHT

Gallagher asked, "What are we going to do, Sheriff?"

"Ride on out of sight, then circle back. Charley's pretty good at slippin' up on a place without bein' seen."

"Yeah," Blackfeather said. "Even though I'm simple-minded."

Satterlee smiled and said, "I figured it was better to insult you than get you shot, and there was probably at least one rifle trained on you from somewhere. I didn't want to start the ball until we knew what the tune was gonna be."

Checking out the Mallory spread was going to delay them to the point that catching up with the gang before they reached Indian Territory would be practically impossible. Satterlee knew that, but he didn't see that they had any choice. The rancher and his family could very well be in danger, and Satterlee's instincts as a lawman wouldn't allow him to ignore that.

Besides, if some of the outlaws were here, taking care of them now would improve the odds that much more in a final showdown. *If* there was a final showdown.

"I'll go back in behind that little rise to the southeast," Charley Blackfeather said when they were out of sight of the ranch. He waved a hand at the low, grassy ridge he'd mentioned.

"I'm comin' with you," Satterlee said.

Blackfeather frowned. "I know you were probably pretty stealthy in your scoutin' days, Sheriff—"

"And I've snuck up on many a herd of buffalo without them knowin' I was there, too," Satterlee broke in. "I know how to move quiet when I have to. Anyway, I intend to stay behind that rise while you slip in the rest of the way. But somebody needs to be close by in case you run into more trouble than you can handle." Satterlee looked around at the other members of the posse and nodded to McCain. "You come along, too."

"Sheriff, I don't know if that's a good idea," Blackfeather said.

"I don't mind," McCain said. "I can be quiet, too. Not as quiet as you two, I'll bet, but I won't give us away."

Rob Gallagher asked, "What about the rest of us, Sheriff?"

"You stay right here," Satterlee said. "If you hear a bunch of shootin', head back in there as fast as you can. And be ready for trouble when you get there."

With the plan in place, Satterlee, Blackfeather, and McCain set out, circling wide to put themselves behind the long ridge that would shield their return to the Mallory ranch. After a mile or so, they had to dismount and lead their horses, because the rise was too shallow to conceal men on horseback. Their hats might have been visible as they bobbed along if they had stayed mounted.

After a while, Blackfeather motioned for them to stop. He handed his reins to the sheriff and said, "I'll crawl up there and take a look, see just how close we are."

Satterlee handed both sets of reins to McCain, took off his hat, and hung it on his saddlehorn.

"You're comin' with me?" Blackfeather guessed.

"That's right."

The two men started up the rise in a crouch, then dropped to hands and knees and finally to their bellies as they crawled the last few feet. At the top, they peered through the grass and Satterlee saw the buildings of the Mallory ranch about three hundred yards away.

As they watched, a man came out of the barn and strode toward the back door of the house.

"That ain't Mallory," Blackfeather said quietly as the man went inside.

"I know. Must be one of the outlaws. Think you can get down there and back without anybody seein' you?"

"There's a chance, anyway."

"If you can find out how many there are, and where they are, we'll have a better chance when we go in."

Blackfeather nodded. "And if I have the chance to slit a throat here and there?"

Satterlee grinned and said, "Hell, go ahead and kill all of 'em if you can, I don't care. Although it might be a good idea to keep one of them alive until we can ask him some questions."

"That was my intent back at the ambush, too, and it didn't work out so good. But I'll do the best I can, Sheriff."

"I know you will, Charley. I wish you luck along the way, too. If we hear a ruckus break out, we'll come a-runnin'."

Blackfeather crawled over the top of the ridge and slithered through the tall grass. Within moments, Satterlee couldn't see him anymore. The grass swayed a little here and there, but with the breezes that swept across the prairie, that was common.

Satterlee looked over his shoulder at McCain and

nodded to let the man know that everything was all right so far. He had sensed a certain amount of tension between Blackfeather and McCain, especially when he'd picked McCain to come along with them on this foray. Maybe McCain didn't care for Indians or black folks—or both—and the Seminole knew that.

It didn't matter to Satterlee how they got along back in town, as long as they were able to work together out here. So far, that hadn't been a problem.

Time dragged. Satterlee looked up at the sun. It was getting on toward mid-afternoon now, and the Danby gang was getting farther away with each passing minute. Unless, of course, they were all holed up down there at the Mallory spread, which seemed unlikely to Satterlee.

That thought had just crossed his mind when he spotted Charley Blackfeather at the rear corner of the barn. Blackfeather bent and slipped between the poles of the corral. He intended to sneak into the barn that way, Satterlee realized. He was impressed that Blackfeather had been able to get down there from up here without ever being visible along the way.

Blackfeather hadn't been inside the barn for more than a minute or two when shots began to roar.

Satterlee twisted around and barked at McCain, "Bring the horses!"

McCain ran up the rise, leading the horses. When he reached the top, the two men swung into their saddles. Satterlee drew his gun and McCain did likewise. The sheriff kicked his mount into a run and thundered down the slope toward the buildings. McCain was close behind him.

The man who had gone inside earlier came running out the back door of the house, saw the riders galloping toward him, and flung up his hand with a gun in it. Smoke and flame erupted from the barrel as he triggered several shots. The range was too great for a handgun, though, and Satterlee knew the man's bullets were falling short. He held his fire, and McCain followed his example.

Charley Blackfeather burst out of the barn, twisting to fire back into the sod building. Blackfeather lost his footing in the hurried action and fell. A man who came out of the barn behind him stopped and drew a bead on him with a revolver.

Derrick McCain suddenly surged past Satterlee as they neared the ranch buildings. The gun in the young man's hand blasted. His shot missed, but it came close enough to the head of the man who was about to fire at Blackfeather that it made him jerk as he squeezed the trigger. The slug kicked up dust several feet to Blackfeather's left.

McCain was practically on top of the gunman by now. He kicked his feet free of the stirrups and dived out of the saddle, crashing into the man and driving him off his feet. Both of them sprawled in the dirt of the yard between the house and the barn.

The man who had come out of the house turned to run, now, as Satterlee closed in on him. He twisted halfway around and flung a shot at Satterlee as he fled. Satterlee thrust his revolver out in front of him and fired.

The bullet slammed into the running man's back and lifted him off his feet. Momentum carried him forward another yard or two before he landed face-first on the ground with his arms flung out on his sides. Satterlee covered the man as he reined in.

Off to the side, McCain struggled with the man he had tackled. The man was bigger than McCain and was able to throw him off. He had dropped his gun, but as he rolled away from McCain he slapped his hand down on the butt and snatched up the weapon. He came up and pointed it toward McCain.

Before he could fire, a grisly thud sounded. Charley Blackfeather's tomahawk had hit him in the back of the head, splitting his skull and driving into his brain. The dying man dropped his gun and pitched forward. After a few grotesque twitches, he lay still.

Satterlee saw that from the corner of his eye as he approached the man he'd shot. That hombre hadn't budged since he fell, and Satterlee was pretty sure he was dead. From the looks of the bloodstain on the back of the man's shirt, Satterlee's bullet had blown right through his heart. It paid to be careful, though, so Satterlee kept his gun pointed at the fallen man until he was able to get a boot toe under his shoulder and roll him over.

The man's eyes stared up sightlessly from a rough, unshaven face.

"Is the other one dead, Charley?" Satterlee called without looking around.

"Dead as he can be," Blackfeather replied.

"Are there any more of 'em?"

"I don't—" Blackfeather began, but before he could finish the back door of the ranch house flew open again, and Ezra Mallory stumbled out.

"Don't shoot!" Mallory cried as he came toward Satterlee, Blackfeather, and McCain. He held his empty hands out in front of him. "There's another one inside! He's got my wife! You've got to help her!"

Satterlee lowered his gun and used his other hand to grab the arm of the panic-stricken rancher.

"Where are they?" he asked.

"Inside and to the right," Mallory said. "He—he's wounded, that's why they left him here, but he's still got a gun—"

Satterlee shoved Mallory toward McCain, who had gotten to his feet and retrieved his gun.

"Keep him here," Satterlee told McCain. The sheriff was growing tired of hysterical husbands and outlaws who hid behind women.

They approached the house cautiously and eased their way inside. Satterlee stood still and listened. He heard some muffled sobs coming from an open door down a short hallway to the right, as Mallory had said. Satterlee silently motioned for Blackfeather to follow, and started along that corridor.

A floorboard creaked under his feet. From inside the room, a man's strained voice called, "I hear you out there! Who's there, damn it? Parker? Drake?"

"Your pards have gone over the Divide, mister," Satterlee replied. "You might as well surrender if you don't want to wind up just like them."

A moment of tense silence went by. Then the man said, "You're a blasted lawman, aren't you? You were with that posse from Wolf Creek."

"That's right. Sheriff G.W. Satterlee. If you surrender—"

"Surrender, hell! So you can take me back and hang me?" A fit of coughing came from the man before he resumed, "Anyway, I won't live that long. So you just come on in here, Sheriff. I got me a hankerin' to kill one more damn star packer before I—before I die."

"Shot in the lungs, aren't you?" Satterlee asked. "I can hear you wheezin' from out here, son. Why should I step in there and let you shoot me when I can just wait out here for you to die?"

Satterlee figured he knew the answer, and sure enough, the outlaw said, "Because if you don't—I'll kill this woman!"

A pained cry came from a female throat. Satterlee's jaw tightened at the sound.

"Let her go," he urged. "Once she's out of there, maybe we can help you. You might not be hurt as bad as you think, and we've got a doctor with us."

That last was a lie, of course. By now, Doc Munro ought to be well on his way back to Wolf Creek with the wounded men. But this low-life owlhoot wouldn't have any way of knowing that.

"Forget it," the man said. "You come in here now, or I—I'll kill her, I swear it."

"Hold on, hold on," Satterlee muttered. He looked back over his shoulder at Blackfeather and motioned for the Seminole to stay where he was. Blackfeather shook his head stubbornly, but Satterlee made a curt gesture to reinforce the order.

"All right," he told the outlaw. "I'm comin' in."

It was only about five steps to the door. Five long steps, Satterlee thought as he started in that direction. His heart slugged hard inside his chest. He had planned to serve as sheriff for a while, maybe two or three more terms if he could keep convincing the voters to elect him, then find himself some nice widow woman to marry and retire. Maybe buy a store or something. He'd spent too blasted long in jobs where, from time to time, he got shot at.

Those plans might not work out. Be a shame if they didn't. But there was nothing he could do, now, except go ahead.

From inside the room, the woman called, "Sheriff, I—I think he's dead!"

Satterlee started to relax and step into the open doorway, then instinct warned him this might be a trick. The outlaw could have whispered to the woman what he wanted her to say, figuring it would make Satterlee drop his guard.

Instead, Satterlee went around the edge of the door low and fast, and when a gun roared deafeningly, he wasn't surprised. The bullet flew over his head, through the door, and ripped a gouge in the wallpaper on the other side of the hall. Satterlee's eyes took in the scene instantly: the bed where the wounded outlaw lay, bloody bandages wrapped around his bare chest, the pale-faced, terrified woman who lay next to him with his left arm looped around her neck, choking her. The outlaw was fumbling at his gun, trying to cock it again after missing his first shot.

With the woman right there, Satterlee didn't want to do any shooting of his own. Instead he leaped across the room and struck the wrist of the man's gun hand with the barrel of his gun. Bone snapped under the impact. The outlaw yelled in pain as his fingers went limp and the gun butt slid out of them.

Satterlee put the muzzle of his gun against the man's forehead. He trembled a little from the urge to pull the trigger. Instead of doing that, he said, "Let the lady go—now!"

The outlaw's arm fell away from the woman's neck. She lunged to her feet and ran from the room, crying hysterically, as the reaction hit her now that she was safe. The sheriff mentally heaved a sigh of relief, himself—he hadn't failed the Mallorys like he did the Haskins family.

Satterlee said, "Only reason I'm not blowin' your brains out right now, mister, is because I don't want to ruin that poor woman's sheets. I figure she's suffered enough just from bein' around you animals."

The outlaw swallowed hard but looked up at Satterlee with defiance in his eyes. "Do it!" he urged. "I'm gonna die anyway!"

"Damn right you are." Satterlee drew in a deep breath. "But not before you tell us where Jim Danby's hideout is."

"You can go to—"

A footstep sounded at the doorway behind Satterlee. "That you, Charley?" he asked.

"Yeah, Sheriff," Blackfeather replied, stepping into the room.

"You see my friend here?" Satterlee asked the outlaw. "He's half black, half Injun. That means there's nothin' he likes better than carvin' on a white man with a knife. Am I right, Charley?"

Blackfeather just grunted in obvious agreement.

"So you can talk, or I'll just walk out of here and leave you with him," Satterlee went on. "I'm bettin' he can find out what I want to know."

Blackfeather stepped up beside Satterlee with his razor-sharp knife in his hand.

Satterlee knew from the terror he saw in the outlaw's eyes that he was going to get the answers he wanted.

****

"First you make out that I'm simple-minded, and then you go around tellin' folks that I'm some sort of crazy savage," Blackfeather said with a faint smile as they rode away from the Mallory ranch. "I'm gonna start to think you don't like me, Sheriff."

"There's nobody I'd rather have along with me on this hunt, Charley," Satterlee told him honestly. "Nobody at all."

The wounded outlaw had died a short time after babbling out the general location of Danby's hideout down in Indian Territory—the Sans Bois Mountains, down in the Choctaw Nation. They got nothing more specific from him. He'd been badly hurt, slowly drowning in his own blood from the bullet he had taken during the raid on Wolf Creek. Mallory had explained that the whole gang had stopped to steal what money and supplies were on hand at the ranch, along with swapping a few of their horses. The wounded man hadn't been able to go on any farther, so Danby figured to leave him there to die. The other two, Parker and Drake, were good friends of his, so they'd offered to stay behind and bury him when he was gone, then catch up to the rest of the gang.

They wouldn't be doing any catching up now. Instead, Mallory would be burying all three of them, although Satterlee told him it would be all right to drag the carcasses well away from the house and leave them for the scavengers. Whichever the rancher decided to do, Satterlee didn't care.

Now, the posse was reunited and moving fast, following the tracks of the remaining outlaws. The odds weren't even yet, but they were closer. Unless there were more members of the gang waiting at the hideout, which was entirely possible, Satterlee reminded himself.

Now that they had a pretty good idea of the general area Danby was bound for, Satterlee was willing to risk riding part of the night. He called a short halt at dusk to let horses and men rest and eat a skimpy supper. When the moon rose and spilled its silvery light across the prairie, they pushed on.

That was the way it continued all night, until finally everyone was too weary to keep going. They rested for several hours then, and took up the chase again early the next morning, as soon as there was enough gray light in the sky for them to see where they were going.

"The tracks are fresher," Charley Blackfeather said after the sun was up. "We made up a little ground on 'em."

"That's good," Satterlee said, but a sinking feeling had begun to grow stronger inside him. He had a decision coming up, and he didn't like it.

At mid-morning, the posse came to a broad, shallow river lined with grassy, sandy banks. Satterlee reined in, rested his hands on the saddlehorn, and leaned forward to ease weary muscles. There was no easing what was in his mind, though.

"That's the Cimarron, isn't it, Charley?"

"Yeah," Blackfeather said. "You know what that means, Sheriff."

It wasn't really a question, but Satterlee said, "Yeah, I do. We crossed over into Indian Territory a while back. I'm out of my jurisdiction now, and that means we ain't legal anymore. I'm entitled to lead a posse through other Kansas counties in pursuit of criminals, but not into the Nations."

"Legal or not," Billy Below said, "we ain't turnin' back, are we, Sheriff?"

"We know where their hideout is now," Rob Gallagher added. "At least, we have a pretty good idea."

"I don't have any choice," Satterlee said, a harsh note

of anger and frustration entering his voice. "I'm sworn to uphold the law. I can't go any farther. This is a matter for somebody else now."

"The Indian police don't have any authority over white men," Blackfeather pointed out. "The only ones who do in Indian Territory are the deputy U.S. marshals who work out of Fort Smith, and that's a long way from here."

"I can get word to them," Satterlee said. "Let them know where Danby's holed up."

"By that time, they may not be there anymore," McCain argued.

"What you're sayin' is true," Satterlee said, "but it doesn't change anything. We're goin' back."

"No," Blackfeather said quietly. "I don't think we are."

Satterlee looked around at the other men. All five of them wore grim, determined expressions, even the normally happy-go-lucky Billy Below.

"I can't let you—" Satterlee began.

"You can't stop us," Sweeney interrupted. "You said it yourself, Sheriff. You don't have any jurisdiction here."

Satterlee's mouth twisted bitterly. They were right. He couldn't stop them from continuing to pursue the outlaws.

And it was eating at his guts that he couldn't join them.

"All right," he said. "But if you go on, you'll be renegades, too, in the eyes of the law."

Blackfeather shrugged. "I reckon we'll risk it." He lifted his reins and turned his horse. "So long, Sheriff."

"You could wish us luck if you wanted to, Sheriff," Gallagher said.

Satterlee just sat his horse in stolid silence as the

others fell in behind Blackfeather and headed south.

Then he whispered, "Good luck," and turned his own horse back to the north. He rode in that direction, shoulders slumped.

CHAPTER NINE

The posse—some of them far too citified to Spike's way of thinking—had surprised him, and proven their mettle when they came up against some of the raiders. There'd already been plenty of blood spilled, and many would have turned tail, but these fellas had all hung on and seemed to still have their teeth sharp.

Since entering the Indian territories they'd ridden hard, covering thirty miles or more while the big scout, Blackfeather, had tracked, sometimes at a lope. They'd traded off dragging two pack mules, each loaded with hard tack, jerky, bacon, dried beans, and extra ammunition. Kansas grass as far as the eye could see had become ravines flanked with red oak, post oak, white cedar, and shortleaf and loblolly pine, with occasional thickets of dogwood lining those cuts hiding creeks. Even with the country getting thicker, but still hard-surfaced, Blackfeather could conjure up more sign while mounted than most men with their nose to the ground. It had been a hell of a lot of miles to cover, considering the rain hadn't blessed the country for a good long time, and the ground was hard as the hubs of hell. But they'd finally staked out the stock and rolled out blankets under some post and red oaks near a trickle of muddy water, downed some jerky and hardtack, and were now watching the moon do a slow climb to the east, each in their own thoughts.

Blackfeather had taken the first watch, and he'd be coming for Spike in a couple of hours, so Spike knew he should be grabbing some shuteye rather than using up the last of his tobacco—but it was a habit, a smoke before turning in. And, hell, tomorrow might be his day to cross over The Divide like a few of the posse already had, should they catch up with Danby and his dirty dogs. Especially if they were outnumbered as much as Spike suspicioned they might be. He was no expert tracker, but the tracks they followed seemed to be made by the better part of a dozen riders, and who knew how many there may be when the gang reached their destination?

Many of the men in Wolf Creek still held deep-seated grudges against those who'd carried the colors of Lee and Jefferson Davis, and Spike didn't hide the truth that he had—in fact, he carried them as a badge of honor, still wearing a butternut kepi to shade his eyes, a kepi with a polished brass Davis Guard medal prominently displayed above the eye shade. The medal was won when a small force of forty-one men turned a fleet of five Union gunboats at Sabine Pass, and saved the day.

Spike had overheard a couple of the boys, Rob Gallagher and Red Myers, badmouthing his kepi earlier on this trek, before the ambush, when they'd slowed to a walk to rest the horses, and gigged his steel gray up alongside Rob Gallagher.

"You two got something against my cover?"

The young man sneered at him. "How come you got to wear that by-God insult to every God-fearing man in town?" Rob asked.

Spike's eyes narrowed, and his voice rang low and

hard. "We got a job of work to do, but I still got time to slip off this animal and make you lisp through some missing teeth."

The young man reddened, then kicked his horse into a trot, as did his trail pard, Red Myers. Spike had taken up a position three horse lengths behind them, content to mind his own business should others not stick their nose into it. Spike couldn't hold a grudge against the tanner Red Myers—he'd gotten his brains blown out at the ambush, after all—but Gallagher, the store clerk, had made it all the way to Indian Territory now, and still seemed to have a chip on his shoulder about Spike's Confederate past.

They'd settled into darkness with only a few clouds marring the clear night, and the stars splattering the open portion of the sky—at least, what could be seen through the red oak canopy. Innumerable stars that seemed to be saying "count us, we dare you to try."

Spike Sweeney leaned against the rough tree trunk and re-lit the carved meerschaum pipe he was never without—he'd traded a sailor out of the pipe, which was adorned with carved head of a full-maned African lion as its bowl. If this manhunt went on much longer, he'd be out of pipe tobacco, and that would be one hell of a note. He'd be better stocked at this point, of course, if he hadn't loaned a couple of bowls full to the Scottish doctor, Munro, on the night after the ambush—but he didn't begrudge it. He'd enjoyed sitting and smoking with Munro, swapping war stories while the doctor's patients slept. Spike was partial to fellow soldiers and meerschaum smokers, no matter which color uniform they'd worn in the war.

He imagined pipe tobacco, here in the territories,

would be hard to come by. Maybe he'd find some Indian tobacco he could trade for, if they came upon some friendly folks who'd left their war paint at home. Finally he knocked the dottle out of his pipe, bagged the meerschaum, and lay his head down on his saddle and its pillow of a folded saddle blanket, pulling the kepi he always wore over his eyes. The smell of horse-lather was soothing to him, after so many years having it as a constant companion.

It seemed he'd barely gotten his eyes closed when he felt a toe nudge his calf. He pushed the kepi back to see Charley bending over him, a finger to his lips.

"I done got the creepies on my backbone," he bent low and whispered. "Either Danby and his boys done doubled back, or we got others out there. Crickets keep quietin' down—an' you got to be up soon anyhow."

Spike knew by the burned down campfire and high moon that he'd been asleep a while. Pulling on his boots, he arose, hooked up the trouser belt that he'd loosened, grabbed one revolver out of its saddle holster, shoved it into the belt, and palmed the other. He moved close to Charley and spoke quietly. "You want I should wake the others?" Rob Gallagher, Billy Below, and Derrick McCain were sleeping hard, two of them snoring loud enough to announce the camp to someone two hundred paces away.

"Nope, if we come on some two-legged critters, gunfire will waken them soon enough. If it's a bunch of four-legged coyotes making the crickets nervous, then no reason. You head out that way—and, Johnny Reb, don't be shooting me should we come back together."

"I never kilt no one didn't need killing, Charley. You try and do the same."

144

Charley faded away, and Spike moved in the direction Charley had indicated. They were moving into a dogwood thicket at a forty-five degree angle. Spike knew the trickle of a muddy creek was only twenty yards into the copse, as he'd watered Hammer there and filled his canteen earlier. Moving quiet was not an easy task, but he toed his way along, having to push brush away as he did so. He'd long ago learned, hunting Texas whitetail and feral hogs, to move a few steps—no more than five—then wait and listen. It was a hunter's habit that had served him well during the war. A man doesn't hear the enemy moving if he's moving himself.

It took him several minutes to make the creek, which was hardly more than a muddy wash, but it was fifteen feet or more of width in the middle of the thicket that was brush free. His first step into the clearing made him pull up short and kneel, as his heel sucked at the mud, and made far too much noise for comfort. On his haunches, he eyed up and down the creek bed.

Patience had never been his long suit, but hunting, men or animals, had taught him his compulsion for moving had to be quelled. Soon, he made out a slight movement up the creek, in the direction he thought Charley must be, and hunkered down even lower and watched and waited. Clouds moved away from the moon, and dim light flooded the creek-bed.

Almost as soon as the clouds moved, Spike made out the shape of a man—only a shadow in the tangle of dogwood—and, as quickly, he caught the glint of metal, then a gurgle, and the man slumped to the mud and muck. For the count of three, sucking sounds came from the body, and the arms flailed. Then Spike realized that while the man was watching him, Charley had slipped up and put a smile in his throat from ear to ear. He could see Charley wiping the blade on his trousers, then re-sheathing it. To Spike's surprise, it seemed that he'd made out a pair of feathers as the man had fallen—an Indian?

The scout made a hand-signal to him to keep moving across the creek, and disappeared.

With a dark streak of blood coloring the creek beneath his strides, he crossed, doing his best to quiet the sucking sound of his boots pulling out of the mud before and after he was in the six-inch-deep stream. In a hundred feet or so, after a half-hour of toeing forward, he came to the edge of the thicket. Charley gave him a low whistle from twenty or more paces away, and he moved, quietly and carefully, to his side.

"Who was he?" Spike asked in a low tone.

"Kiowa. And he wasn't alone."

"So, where are the rest of them?"

"Skeedaddled. See that," Charley pointed to the ground.

Spike kneeled and studied the edges of some prints, but couldn't make out what it was. He arose and shrugged.

"Cattle. Looks like a band of Kiowa wandered over the Cimarron and rustled up a couple of dozen head of beef. I'll bet they think we're doggin' their trail."

"So, now we got to worry about a band of savages—pardon the description."

"Hell," Charley said, "they *are* savages." He offered a tight smile, then continued. "They'll take your hair sooner than sit down to a back strap off'n one of those beeves."

"You left one ol' boy lay back there."

146

"I did, and I imagine when they get wind that one of their own have gone missing—odds are, there'll be hell to pay. We ain't heard near the end of it."

"Maybe we'd better stand a double watch the rest of the night?"

"Sounds right, I'll take another two hours along with you, then we'll wake Gallagher and Billy, and let McCain sleep. We'd all better make sure our powder is dry come dawn."

"We better high tail it back. The rest of his band could have flanked us and hit the camp."

They made their way back to the creek much faster than they'd come, dragging the dead Kiowa behind rather than leaving him to be found. No one else stirred, nor had the band of Kiowa taken the scalps of the sleeping men.

All of them were beaned up, coffee filled, and mounted as the sky to the east began to color up. They'd left the corpse of the Kiowa brave in as presentable a position as possible for a man with a wide crimson smile from ear to ear and the front of his backbone showing through his gaping sliced throat—his old percussion rifle and knife lay across his chest as if he were ready to take a long trip to meet his Maker. Spike and the other three had talked hard to keep Charley from taking the man's scalp, figuring it might anger the band less. They only hoped that driving the small herd of beeves on was more important to the band than waiting for their missing *compadre* to show up. They hoped, but doubted it.

Charley took up the point, since he was doing the tracking, with Billy Below, Derrick McCain, Rob Gallagher following. Spike Sweeney rode drag, figuring himself the most experienced of those who'd fought in a group. He knew to watch his back trail and flanks almost as much as ahead.

Then the outlaws' trail disappeared, hidden under that of several unshod horses and a couple of dozen beeves. Charley reined up and let the others come alongside.

"We're still on the outlaw trail, but we are also riding into double trouble. Watch careful and help me spot if these trails split. Let's hope they do, and we can fight shy of following the Kiowa." He pointed to each of them in turn. "And ever' damn one of you watch for ambush. This thick cover would hide a herd of buffs."

They all were relieved when they pulled up into some low hills and the cover thinned to spotted post oaks—at least, until they spotted a dozen Kiowa quietly sitting their mounts on the skyline a quarter mile ahead.

Billy Below had to call out to Charley, as the scout was concentrating on the trail. "There's a thunder pot load of trouble up ahead."

Again, Charley pulled rein and waited for the others to come even.

"Five against a dozen ain't good odds," Billy said quietly when he reined up.

"Rotten, fact is," Charley said. "Won't do much good to run—we been pushin' these horses too hard. I'm going on up alone to parlay. And that's not all of them, as they would have some watching that herd they rustled, wherever they got 'em hid out. You boys get your ready on."

Billy looked at him skeptically. "You ain't thinkin' of changin' sides are you?"

Charley stared him down, then said, "Well, Billy boy, if I do, then the odds will be some worse, won't they? If you don't know which way my stick floats by now, you never will." He nudged his horse forward and left them all to wonder, then he turned back and spoke over his shoulder as he rode away. "'Course, your hair would look just fine on my coup stick." He laughed, and gigged his horse into a lope.

Spike couldn't help but laugh as well, but it was short-lived and nervous. He looked the country over as Charley moved away, then spoke up. "There's a little thicket up the hill a ways—there," he pointed, "with some admirable rocks for cover. There's a green spot there, maybe a little spring or seep. Should it come to that, break for there."

"Who made you straw boss?" Gallagher muttered.

Spike eyed him carefully, then said in a low tone, "Tell you what, young fella, you ride on out of here hell for leather on that beat up nag of yours. Maybe you can lead them away from the rest of us, and while they're taking your hair, eatin' your liver, and divvying up your folderol, maybe we can sneak out unmolested."

Gallagher reddened, but said nothing more.

"The rocks it is," Derrick McCain agreed. "Maybe we should wander that way?"

"Let's see how it plays out with Charley. We don't want to make those folks nervous while Charley is parlaying with them. We got three hundred or more paces on 'em, should we make a run for it. That should give us time to get hunkered down and tucked behind cover a'fore they get on us."

They sat their mounts casually as Charley reached the band. It soon became obvious by the hands flying with sign talk that the parlay wasn't going well. However, in moments, Charley spun his horse and trotted back to join them— followed by two Kiowa braves. The braves reined up twenty paces back.

Charley wasted no time instructing them. "Take half the supplies out of the panniers and load what you can in your saddle bags. I've given them the mules and what we can't haul."

"The hell you say," Billy Below snapped, and Derrick McCain and Rob Gallagher chimed in.

"Hold on," Spike said. "You want to give them your hair or a couple of butt ugly mules and some dried meat? Get the ammunition, for sure."

"You want it, you get it, *straw boss*," Rob Gallagher groused, and sat unmoving.

Spike, thinking it no time for long drawn out discussion, dismounted and headed for the mules. Derrick McCain leapt off his animal, dropped the reins, and followed. In moments they had the panniers half unloaded, then Spike took up both lead ropes and led the animals to the waiting braves, who took them up and without looking back, trotted away, yelping in triumph.

Spike remounted and reined over beside Charley. "Did they ask about their chum?"

"Nope, and I sure-as-hell's-hot didn't bring it up. I did get a peek at a fresh scraped hide one of them had thrown over the rump of his horse. It had a Crown-W brand. Old man Sparkman will be spittin' sparks when he figures out he's missing two dozen or more head of prime beef."

Spike shook his head and smiled wryly. Ward Sparkman owned the largest spread in the vicinity of Wolf Creek, and he was a hard man, not having built the biggest ranch in the area by handing stock over to every passing band of Indians. The Kiowa could have chosen easier prey. Spike knew Sparkman well, having done lots of work for him—most of the Crown-W spread was in

Taylor County, and Sparkman's house was twenty miles southwest of Wolf Creek. Spike knew that the old man would chase this band to the ends of the earth had they driven off one of the geese he kept in a pond near the house, much less two or three hundred dollars worth of stock. And they left a trail wide as a St. Louis street. These Kiowa would rue the day…

"They did sign where the outlaws were headed," Charley said, "and where I can pick up the trail east of here. Seems they saw a passel of them, eight or so, only yesterday. Let's get what we can stowed in our saddle bags and pound trail before these dirty Kiowa go to missing their man and ride back to find him."

Spike was feeling good about what Charley had accomplished. They rode on at a lope until they picked up the trail of shod horses again, then had to walk their horses before they collapsed. They made camp early on the crown of a low hill.

"I don't see what the hell we're stoppin' for," Gallagher said, "when we're so close to those killers we can almost smell 'em."

"I reckon that's why I'm a cowboy and you're a store clerk," Billy Below said with a grin. "If we don't rest these hosses we'll be walkin' through the Nations. And as long as they're resting, we might as well do the same."

"They've got horses, too," Charley added. "And they've already slowed their pace considerable, their tracks tell me that. They probably figure they're home free in Indian Territory and no posse can follow 'em— plus, so far as they know, Wes Hammond and the others that lagged behind to ambush the posse either wiped us out or sent us packing back to Wolf Creek, and are bringing up the rear now for the main group. So they'll be restin' their horses tonight, same as us, and we'll set out in the morning in a much bigger hurry than they're in. I figure we'll close in on 'em sometime late tomorrow."

"God willin' and the creek don't rise," Spike Sweeney said. "And these creeks don't look like they've rose in a long spell."

Billy laughed at the comment, but Gallagher scowled and walked off.

Spike shook his head, and spoke in a low voice so that only Billy could hear. "That boy's showed a lot of pluck on this trip," he said. "I don't reckon none of us would've expected him to handle his self as well as he has. But he sure as hell has a burr under his saddle."

"Yeah," Billy agreed. "It ain't like him, neither, I've always knowed him to be good-natured. Of course, everybody's good-natured around me, on account of I'm so blamed charming. Maybe all this shootin' and gettin' shot at is too new to him."

Spike grunted. "Wish I could say the same."

CHAPTER TEN

Spike rolled up as the first light turned the eastern sky to brass, and noticed that Charley had already done so. The scout's gear, including his saddle, was piled ready to pack on the back of his mount, but he was nowhere to be seen. Spike went ahead and poked up the fire. They'd soaked beans overnight in a pair of canteens, so Spike dug out a pot he knew Charley carried and got the beans to cooking while he carved some fat slices of bacon and, using his skillet, got them to browning and spittin' fat. The other men were slow to rise, and Spike saw no reason to hurry them, as the beans weren't done and Charley was still down the hill somewhere.

He was just draining the beans—while the other three had walked out of camp to relieve themselves—when he heard some shouting coming from down the slope, where an elm lined ravine cut across the meadow. Spike kept his eyes peeled at the area, while he added some salt and bacon grease to the beans.

In a heartbeat, he set the frying pan full of bacon and the pot full of beans down beside the fire to keep warm. Charley broke out of the ravine below at a dead run. Spike hustled for his Austrian and took up a prone position beside a granite outcropping, a shoulder of which would serve as a rest for the heavy-barreled weapon. It was a good thing he did, as Charley was still a hundred yards from camp when two Kiowa crashed out of the ravine on horseback, firing handguns as they came.

By the time Spike had sighted in on the leading rider, the man was only a hundred paces from Charley and closing fast. The big Austrian roared and bucked in Spike's grip, and the leading Kiowa's horse buckled under him, throwing the rider hard. He figured it better to stop the rider than try and kill him. The other three of his compatriots had made it to their weapons, and gunfire barked as the second Kiowa spun his horse and, laying low across the animal's neck, wisely galloped for the elms.

Charley stopped cold, turned, eyed the situation, and strode back to the fallen Kiowa—who, although knocked senseless, was trying to regain his feet. Charley easily relieved the man of his revolver, which must have been emptied, and shoved it in his own belt. The big Bowie Charley carried was as quickly in hand, and he shanked it to the hilt, deep into the Indian's gut, allowed him to fall, then took his hair with three clean slices of the knife. He wiped the knife blood-free on the Indian's breechcloth, which he wore over tattered trousers. An old percussion rifle had been thrown clear and Charley walked over, picked it up, examined it, then smashed it across a nearby chunk of granite. Only then did he turn and stride casually up the hill to the camp. He'd almost reached the crest when gunfire broke out from the line of trees, kicking up dirt all around him. He took up a trot and soon dropped down beside where Spike hunkered down behind his ledge, reloading the Austrian.

"You couldn't sleep, or what?" Spike asked him, as a couple of shots from the ravine below sung over their heads. McCain, Gallagher and Billy returned fire.

"Don't trust those damn dirty Kiowa," Charley said. "And a good thing. They was working up a head of steam down below that ravine, figuring on divvying up the rest of our goods and critters come sun up." Charley turned his attention to the others for a moment. "Don't waste your powder until you got a good target."

"How come they saw you?" Spike chided.

"They didn't. Damn crow got to yappin' at me."

"Thought you Indians could talk to the wild things?" Spike continued to chide.

"He must have been a Kiowa crow," Charley said, "He paid me no mind."

That brought a chuckle from Spike, but he became serious once more as he continued to watch the Indian Charley had scalped. The man was now on his knees, one hand on his profusely bleeding scalp, one on his stomach wound.

"He's not dead," Spike said.

"Didn't mean to kill him quick. It be fine if he suffers a while. He's a Kiowa."

Spike shook his head. "Not fine. I don't care if he's a skunk." He picked up the Austrian, and at one hundred-and-fifty yards, blew the man's head apart. "Won't suffer now," Spike said.

"You wasted good lead on him," Charley said.

"I wouldn't let a rattlesnake die that hard. I saw too many men, gut shot, crying for their mamas out in some frying-pan-hot field."

"Speaking of frying pans," Charley said, looking around. "Is that bacon I smell?"

"Damn sure is, if you can get to it. I guess we'd better divide it up. May be our last meal." Spike motioned to a meadow five hundred yards down the hill, where at least fifteen Kiowa braves had gathered.

"Guess we should eat quick," Charley said, "then figure out how to best defend this damned ol' dry hill."

The firing from below had stopped, so Charley bravely rose and walked to the fire, retrieved a hand full of bacon and some hardtack Spike had laid out there, and returned and handed it to Spike.

"Obliged," Spike said, then added, "they've split up in four bunches of three or four each. I imagine they are going to try and flank the hill. You may think I'm crazy, but we should turn the stock out before they take it on themselves to shoot them down." He rose and headed for the horses while Charley moved to join the other men at the fire and food.

"What's he up to?" Rob Gallagher asked.

"Turning the horses out," Charley said.

"The hell he is," Rob snapped, as he strode away to head Spike off.

"Hey!" Charley yelled, and Rob stopped and turned back.

"You're a greenhorn at this. Spike knows what he's doing."

"But—"

"No buts. Get back here and bean up. It could be a long while before you'll have a chance again. Loose horses is better than dead horses, don't ya know."

As Spike drove four of the horses away, and only held onto Hammer, his steel gray, Rob Gallagher reddened and started to stomp toward him. Charley swept a moccasin clad foot under the retreating man, and Gallagher hit the ground hard, rolled to his side, and gave Charley a look that could kill.

"He's keeping his own damn horse and running our'n

away," Gallagher sputtered.

Charley shook his head, sighed, and explained, "He's risking his horse, while letting ours live. And should any of us live, we'll need a mount to round the others up. Eat your breakfast, then make peace with your Maker, for it's a good day to die. In about ten minutes, we'll be totally surrounded."

Spike found a place fairly well sheltered from any fire coming from lower down the hill. He staked the steel gray out and moved to his gear. He removed a pair of hobbles from his haversack then turned to the others. "Any of you got hobbles?"

All of then shook their heads or shrugged.

Spike continued, "Any of you got a lead rope in your saddle bags?"

"I got a piece of rope," Gallagher said grudgingly.

"Fish it out."

Spike took it, returned to the steel gray, hobbled his front feet with the leather hobbles, forced the animal down on his side, then tied his back feet, keeping him down out of the line of fire unless the Indians got high on the hill, which would most likely no longer matter as it would mean they were in camp, and they'd all be dead.

Then men took up positions at each quarter of the compass. Each of them had more than one weapon, Charley with his Army Colt and a scarred Winchester Yellowboy studded with brass tacks, McCain with a pair of Navy Colts, and Rob Gallagher with a '66 Winchester Yellowboy. Gallagher's rifle was bright and shiny—it had probably never been fired. It had been loaned to him by his boss for this venture. The store clerk also had a pair of rare newly acquired baby LeMats—he'd relieved one of the dead outlaws of that valuable load. He was

157

now a squad of men all by himself, when it came to fire power. The Smith and Wesson he'd left town with was tucked into his waistband. Spike laid his two Rigdon and Ainsley's in easy reach, his double barrel stage guard's scattergun and its twenty double-aught brass shells in the crack of rock, and settled down to watch his quadrant.

At the moment, as the sun climbed, it was the only enemy in sight. The humidity seemed to keep up with the temperature as they all began to wipe the sweat from their eyes. Spike finally rose and left his post for a moment, took his canteen, and wet Ham's lips. The big gray was no virgin when it came to being in prone position on a battlefield, but it was usually with Spike holding him down, lying across him to lay fire on an approaching enemy. The big horse didn't like being tied down, and whinnied his objection upon occasion.

"Here they come," Charley shouted, and Spike sprinted back to his position. Charley continued, "Don't get in a hurry, they'll run some feints first to try and get us to burn powder."

And he was right. They rode to within a hundred yards, then broke away, dropping to the sides of their mounts away from the hilltop.

They disappeared back into the trees or the ravine, or behind a ledge where they couldn't be seen from above. It was a quarter hour more before they came again.

Charley yelled again, "Let them get to fifty paces before you fire. They'll make three or four of these mock charges before they hit us hard."

Spike was happy to comply, until one of the Kiowa reined his horse up almost two hundred yards down the hill and sat, defiantly, shaking his rifle at the men above.

Taking a deep breath, quieting his heart, Spike lay

down on the man. The Austrian roared and blew enough smoke that Spike couldn't see the result, until he heard Rob Gallagher speak up. "Damn good shot, damn good."

Spike saw the man's rider-less paint horse galloping away, and the crumpled body of the Indian being dragged off by two of his fellows. In seconds, they were out of sight in the ravine.

"Dirty Kiowa, dog dead," Charley Blackfeather said with a tight smile. "Odds getting better." He barely got it out before gunfire rained down on them. The Indians were trying a new tactic, setting up in the trees and rocks to try and pick them off.

"This could be a damned long affair," Charley said. In moments, he shouted out. "How much water you fellas got?"

"I got most of one canteen," Spike said. "I used the other to soak the beans."

"I got a canteen and a goat gut full," Billy Below said. "Maybe a quart and a half."

"A canteen and a quart of Who Hit John," Rob Gallagher called out.

"I guess I should have filled up," Derrick McCain said. "I only got a half a canteen."

"It'll be hell to pay, come tomorrow afternoon," Charley said, and for the first time, Spike thought he detected worry in the big man's tone. He studied the hillside below his position. "Let's hope these Kiowa start missing their women."

"Will they come at night?" Spike asked.

"Doubt it, but who knows? If they keep us here until late tomorrow, we may have to kill that gray of yours and chow down on him. Hot wet meat's better than no moisture at all."

"The hell you say," Spike snarled. "I'll ride him down there and take them all on before any of us put our teeth to him."

Charley spoke without looking over, still staring down the hill. "We'll see if you say that tomorrow afternoon. Pray to that Lutheran God of yours for rain."

"Humph," Spike managed.

****

They didn't come again that afternoon. However, with the dark, they could see fires below on all four quadrants. The stars shone bright all night, and dawn came without a cloud in the sky. The good Lord would be no help with thirst quenching rain. They'd nursed their water, but all of them were sweating their internal moisture away throughout the warm night, and none of them slept. With only five of them, and each only able to watch a section of the hill, there could be no sleeping.

They were able to have beans for breakfast, but Spike wished he hadn't salted them. They were not thirst quenching. They were down to a canteen of water each, and that was gone by noon, then, even knowing it would probably compound their thirst, they passed the bottle of whiskey around, killing half of it off. As Charley suggested, they were better off with the moisture in their gut than in their canteens.

The Kiowa waited until the sun was overhead, then began the feinting tactic again. As they had ample ammunition, and would run out of water long before they ran out of powder, the men began taking pot shots at the riders at a hundred yards distant. The Indians rode hard, staying low in the saddle, very tough targets at a swift gallop. Still, the men felt they'd hit two more and knew they'd hit one solid, as his horse had drug him over the hill, his head bouncing along the rough ground.

"It's about time," Charley said.

"Time for what?" Gallagher called out from the opposite side of their position.

"They'll either give up, or charge hard. And the Kiowa don't give up. They'll figure we're damn tired and can't see worth a hoot in this bright sun, with the sweat and all, and knowing we probably didn't sleep a blink."

As if he were reading the enemies' minds, they suddenly came at once, from all directions, at least four of them coming at every man.

"Hold until you're sure!" Charley shouted.

Spike dropped a man out of the saddle with the long-shooting Austrian almost as soon as he'd topped the rise, and rather than try to reload, grabbed up his revolvers and began firing offhand. McCain and Charley were firing a slow steady pace, considering the Indians would be on them in another ten seconds, and Gallagher was firing the Yellowboy as fast as he could lever it.

All but one of the Indians turned, firing over their shoulders as they retreated. The one that didn't turn tail was riding hard in Spike's quadrant at a full gallop, low in the saddle, a revolver in hand.

Spike rose and fired once, missing, then both revolvers snapped on empty chambers. He clambered for the scattergun—the Indian was only twenty paces away, coming hard, screaming heathen curses. Spike barely got his weapon up as they both fired at the same time.

I'm kilt, Spike thought—he felt as if his chest had caved in, and he was blown to his back as the Indian's mount leapt over him. His vision faded, then he felt the others lifting him. The half-empty whiskey bottle touched his lips, but he was coughing, coughing too hard to drink.

His eyes cleared and he felt for the wound, surprised he still could, as he knew half his heart had been blown away. He grasped his chest, then realized his meerschaum was smashed in his shirt pocket. He coughed again, then ran a hand inside his shirt, picking shards of pipe out of his chest, but finding no hole spurting blood.

"Damned if you ain't still alive," Charley managed.

"Damned—damned if I—" he coughed again, "damned if I ain't," Spike said, then sat up. He could see that both barrels of double-aught had blown the Kiowa brave out of the saddle, and he didn't fare nearly so well as Spike had.

"I think—I think I done broke a rib," Spike managed, rubbing his chest. "And that was a fine pipe, the likes of which I'll never find again. Som'bitch kilt my lion." He couldn't help but grin stupidly.

"Son of a bitch," Charley said. "You're worried about the damned pipe? You're lucky you got a heart and a lung." He began to laugh as Spike collected himself. Then Spike stood, still rubbing his chest, and gathered up his weapons.

He quickly reloaded the Austrian again, catching a lot of deep breaths as he loaded the rest of his arsenal.

"Will they come again?" Spike finally yelled at Charley, as he retook his position with the Austrian again on the hard rock shoulder.

"Odds are."

"Good," Spike said, "I'm out of water anyway. Let's end this, my damn chest hurts."

But they didn't come. And they didn't leave.

Night fell, and the campfires below teased them

again. They decided to set pickets, as they had to have sleep. Two would sleep, and two would pace from position to position, taking two-hour watches.

Morning came—to their dismay, another beautiful morning, warm and welcoming. Scissortails winged overhead, dodging in and out of a flight of crows. Had they not all had swelling tongues and throats you could strike a Lucifer upon, it would have been a morning to shout about.

Again a barrage of gunfire erupted, this time as soon as it was light enough to see. It went on, with sporadic fire until mid-morning.

Finally, Charley shouted over to Spike, "I'm ready to cut that gray's throat and roast us up some equine backstrap."

"You got enough folks shootin' at you already, Charley," Spike snapped. "We'll finish off that quart of whiskey long before we roast my horse."

Billy Below gave them a quiet laugh, then said, "Oh, yeah, and we'll be fine shots cross-eyed drunk. I'd as soon down my fourth of what's left right before I'm being scalped."

As he finished the sentence, all hell broke loose, and the barrage from below seemed to erupt into a crescendo of gunfire, each shot melding into the next until it seemed constant. Far more than they'd had at any time before.

Each of the men set up, ready to take on the charging Indians. To their surprise, a few of them broke from the cover of the trees, riding their way, but firing back over their shoulders. They broke away to circle the hill.

Spike rubbed his eyes, not believing what he was seeing. The Indians rounded the hill, not trying to crest their position, and more than one tumbled from his horse in the process.

What the hell was happening?

The men stared from their lofty position, waiting as the growing silence compounded their curiosity.

In moments, at least twenty riders began sifting out of the trees, and these men were in wide-brimmed hats, riding the pommeled and horned saddles of cowmen.

Spike, Charley, Rob, Billy, and Derrick rose, a little shaky from the lack of water, and watched gratefully as the men stopped at each fallen rider to make sure the Kiowa had gone to meet his Maker, then continued on up the hill.

A barrel-chested man was in the lead, white hair to his shoulders, his gray porkchop whiskers askew and bone-white handlebar mustache drooping, his blue eyes cold, hard and unflinching. He dismounted, seemingly having been more comfortable in the saddle than on foot, and walked over and extended a ham-sized well-calloused hand to Spike.

"Mister Sweeney," he said, "I appreciate your keeping this band of hostiles busy until we could catch up and take care of business."

"Our pleasure, Mister Sparkman." Spike croaked. "Glad to see you, but to be honest, we're even more pleased to see your canteens."

CHAPTER ELEVEN

"What're you fellas doing out here?" Sparkman asked. None of them answered immediately. They were all thirstily drinking the welcome, if warm, water that Sparkman's men carried.

Finally, Derrick drew a sleeve across his mouth and said, "We're after a gang of outlaws, Mister Sparkman. They're what's left of Danby's men. Rode into Wolf Creek a few days ago and shot up the town. We aim to track 'em down." He glanced around at Sparkman's men. None of them would meet his eyes. It was plain they'd rather go after the Kiowas than join in the hunt for Jim Danby's crew.

"We could sure use some help, if you can spare—" Spike began, but Sparkman cut him off.

"Sorry, Sweeney. We've got our own rat killin' to attend to. I can't spare anyone for your manhunt right now—not until we catch up with these Kiowas and teach them a lesson about stealing from Ward Sparkman. Sorry bastards. This is the third time this month they've dared to try it."

"But," Billy said, "we're talking about Danby's men killing people! You're just wanting to stop the Kiowas from rustling your cattle—"

"I'm afraid it's a matter of pride, son. Pride and money. I've lost at least fifty head of beeves, just this month. I'm not going to lose any more."

He turned in his saddle and motioned to his men. "Let's find these gentlemen's horses so they can be on their way, shall we? They have business to attend to, and so do we."

****

Less than half an hour later, the scattered horses had been gathered, and Sparkman and his men had started off after Stone Knife's Kiowa raiders once more.

"Where're we gonna fill up our canteens?" Billy Below asked, watching them ride toward the west.

"We're not far from the Arkansas River," Derrick answered. "No more'n prob'ly ten miles or so."

"Not far, if you ain't bein' shot at by a passel of Kiowas," Spike agreed.

"Can't believe Sparkman couldn't spare us a few of his men," Rob muttered. He settled his hat on his head, but it did nothing to shade the disgusted look he shot the retreating riders' backs.

Charley shrugged. "We'll manage without 'em." He glanced at Derrick with a faint grin. "Long as we remember to fill up our canteens."

Derrick's quick anger faded as he realized Charley was teasing. He'd made a mistake he wouldn't repeat again—not in the unforgiving terrain of Indian Territory, and especially, not in this July heat.

"Let's head for the river, boys," Spike said easily. "Canteen fillin's gotta be the first order of business. Then, we'll head out after the bastards. We still have some daylight left to follow this bloody trail we're on."

****

166

They'd watered up and started back toward the southeast again, following a track along the Arkansas in the area where Stone Knife had said the eight outlaws were when the Kiowas ran into them. Charley had picked up their trail easily—they'd made no effort to hide it.

After an hour or so, Charley rode close to Derrick and offered him a piece of jerky. "You never got much of a breakfast this mornin', Cherokee," Charley said quietly. Derrick shot him a quick questioning look, and Charley laughed. "Don't take offense white boy. I ain't gonna spill your secret."

Derrick took the dried beef with a nod of thanks.

"I don't have a secret, Blackfeather. It's all in your mind. One of your damn peyote visions or somethin'."

"Oh, I think you got plenty of secrets. You know the place where they're headed, don't you?" Charley asked, dropping the sore subject. "Danby's man that died back at the farmhouse—he talked some before he passed. Said there was a couple of places Danby's gang could be headed for in the San Bois Mountains. Course, I had to persuade him a little—but I think he told the truth, in the end." He paused, then said, "Stone Knife, he said he heard one of 'em mention the San Bois Mountains too."

"Yeah," Derrick answered after a brief pause. "I'm only hoping we catch them before they make it."

"Got any idea exactly where they might head to in those mountains, McCain?"

Derrick nodded reluctantly. "There's a place there they run to where they can hole up forever if need be. It's near the top of one of the tallest peaks. Got a waterfall that runs right by the camp, so there's always fresh water. They call it Demon's Drop."

Charley nodded. "I've heard of the place. Not just

used by Danby's men, either. It's a meeting place and hideout for others, too. They say there's no way in, alive, unless you're invited. I don't reckon we're invited." He smiled.

Derrick shook his head. "No. Well, one of us would've been, if I hadn't mutinied out there on that field that day tryin' to save your ass."

"Sometimes, it just doesn't pay to say 'no'." Charley glanced behind him to be sure Billy, Rob and Spike were following through the dense foliage. "I'm sure as hell glad you did, that day, even though it 'bout got you murdered."

"We survived. Both of us." Derrick shifted in the saddle, his hand moving up over his shirt front, over the old scar that lay three inches from his heart. He'd survived, all right, but he didn't know how. Or why.

****

The sun began to relent, the sky beyond where they rode off to their right turning a tangerine color that slid into pink.

"What's that noise?" Billy asked, riding up alongside Derrick. Derrick reined up and gave a short whistle. Charley, who'd ridden a few yards ahead, turned to backtrack.

"Sounds like rushing water," Rob said as he caught up to the group, cocking his head to the side.

"We've moved west of the Arkansas a couple of miles," Derrick explained, "But we're a stone's throw from the Canadian. And a few miles from where we'll cross it, there are some rapids where the river forks off into two branches—the main fork and the north fork.

North fork is nearly as big as the main river itself, and as powerful, in places. That fast runnin' water is what you're hearing, Billy."

"I'm guessing you know where to cross," Spike said. He looked thoughtful for a moment before he added, "Did they cross? Do we know that for certain?"

Charley looked at Derrick, clearly letting him know it was up to him to tell as much, or as little, as he wanted the others to know. Another one of your secrets, his expression plainly stated.

"McCain's family came from around these parts," Charley said easily. "He knows of a place up in the San Bois Mountains, Demon's Drop, that's a known hideout for desperadoes like Danby's men. We think they might be headed there."

Spike nodded. "Gotta get 'em before they make it that far, then." He gave Derrick a long look. "Been a long time since your family left this area, hasn't it?"

Derrick didn't flinch. "Some things, you never forget."

"We can make camp on this side of the Canadian. Cross it in the morning," Billy said, breaking the tension.

"No," Charley and Derrick said in unison. Then, Derrick fell silent as Charley explained. "We don't know what the night might bring. I've been noticing how thick the air feels. Could be a storm movin' in. If that happens, it could make the river a bitch to cross."

Spike wiped a hand across his forehead, then settled the kepi back in place. "A storm? I don't see how. Feels like we've been riding through hell."

"Especially earlier, when we thought those Kiowas had us," Rob muttered.

Derrick hid a smile. And me with a half-empty canteen. "We'll find a good crossing and have that behind us, no matter what comes along in the morning."

* * * *

The river was low, due to the heat of midsummer, and the lack of rain for so many weeks. From the parched look of the land, Derrick thought, there must not have been any rain for at least a month or more. The farther south they rode, the more marked the signs of the drought were. The low river, though, was a blessing for them as it provided easy crossing after riding no more than a half-mile back upstream to the east.

They crossed with the water barely coming higher than stirrup-level, the horses never losing their footing. Derrick removed his Yellowboy from the saddle scabbard, as did the others with their longarms, to avoid the unknown depths of the water they were crossing.

Once on the south bank of the river, they all dismounted. Billy said, "I'm ready to make camp right here, right now."

But Charley's head was up, his dark eyes scanning the clearing on the bank where they stood, and the trees beyond. "I smell smoke," he said softly.

Derrick nodded his agreement. "Let's find out if we might finish our business tonight. I'd sleep a hell of a lot better knowin' we could get up and start home in the mornin'."

"Agreed," said Spike. He nodded toward the west. "Do we split up?"

Charley shook his head. "No. We need to stick together till we see what we're up against. I'm not sure

170

Danby's men would stop here."

"We did," Rob said, not understanding.

"Yes," Charley answered, "but we are trailing them, youngblood. And I think they know it. I'm not sure they'd stop for anything. They'll be running as if the devil's at their heels, if they know we're still behind them."

Derrick gave a short laugh. "Same thing, in this case, Blackfeather. Once we catch them, they may wish it was only Satan, himself, after them."

"Speaking of Satan," Spike breathed, "who the hell is that?"

****

A man sat, unmoving, on a large black horse at the western edge of the clearing.

"And that?" Rob added, looking past Derrick's shoulder at the fringe of woods to the south where another mounted horseman sat watching them.

In the early twilight shadows, Derrick couldn't be certain, but they looked Cherokee, and in the dimming light, he caught glint of silver on the chest of the short rider when he'd turned to look behind him. Lighthorse officers, he hoped.

"Halito," he called. Hello.

They both rode forward, stopping a few feet away from the Wolf Creek posse, their faces impassive.

"What business do you have?" the short rider asked.

Charley gave Derrick a look that said, 'you take this.' Had to be because of his "Cherokee face", Derrick thought wryly.

"We're looking for some men," Derrick answered,

171

walking a few steps toward the two. Somehow, he knew Charley and Spike had him covered, whether the two younger men of their party had the sense to or not.

"What men?" asked the taller, more dour looking of the two.

"They killed some of our people," Derrick said. "Robbed the savings and loan, up north—in Kansas."

"Long way. You are here to recover the money?" Sour-Face asked.

"We're here to see justice done for the people they murdered," Derrick said evenly. "Several men. A woman. A child. Even our animals." He took another step forward, and both men brought their rifles to bear, training them at his chest. His stomach churned, as he remembered the last time he'd looked down a gun barrel; the flash and roar, the ungodly pain that had ripped through his flesh. He made sure his hands were well away from the Navy Colts he wore. "Are you lighthorse?"

After a moment, the shorter one answered. "Yes." He nodded at their horses. "Mount up and ride with us. Our camp is not too far. We have a U.S. Deputy Marshal in our company." He watched closely to see what effect his words might have on them. A test, Derrick knew, to see if they were telling the truth. Would they fight, or would they ride into camp and face a U.S. Marshal? Were they after the outlaws, or were they the outlaws themselves?

Derrick gave him a brief nod, but his heart sank as he remembered Satterlee's words before he'd left the posse. "If you go on, you'll be renegades, too, in the eyes of the law."

They were out of their jurisdiction, and none of them were truly lawmen. They only had one hope of

172

continuing on after Danby's men. Whoever this Deputy was, maybe he would consider joining up and stringing along with the men from Wolf Creek, making their cause his, as well—and they would become his posse.

All of them mounted up, and they rode slowly through the darkening woods. The shorter Cherokee officer kept pace with Derrick at the front, the stone-faced, taller one at the back with Charley. Spike, Billy and Rob rode in between.

It wasn't more than three-quarters of a mile until they reached the lighthorse camp. There was a small clearing beside a creek that flowed from a freshwater spring near the river, and they'd gotten a fire burning with a dinner of fish and fry bread going. Two other lighthorsemen and the U.S. Deputy Marshal sat back from the fire, away from the heat.

As they rode in, the shorter Cherokee officer called out a 'safe' greeting, and the others stood up, setting their cups and plates on the ground.

The Wolf Creek men dismounted as the lighthorsemen swung down and spoke to the others in Cherokee, one of them translating in English to the deputy marshal. The voice of the translator sounded somehow familiar to Derrick, though the tone was not. But when the man turned to face him, recognition struck, swift and certain.

"Carson?" he said in a disbelieving whisper. "Carson Ridge?"

The translator's black eyes met Derrick's.

Derrick took a step toward him, then another. "My God, I can't believe—"

"I thought I'd never see you—"

They both broke off, but Ridge closed the few steps

between them and put his hands on Derrick's shoulders. A broad grin crossed his face.

"Welcome, brother. You are welcome."

"What the hell's goin' on?" Spike asked Charley from where they stood to the side of the two men.

Charley suppressed a smile at the shock that was evident on Derrick's features. Obviously, the McCain family's move to Kansas hadn't been totally motivated by politics. When Derrick and Ridge stood together, even in the flickering light and shadows cast by the distant fire, there was no doubt they shared the same blood. Andrew McCain wasn't Derrick's father. McCain wasn't even rightly Derrick's name. McCain and Ridge may have had different mothers, Charley thought, but they'd damn sure had the same father.

"Brother," Ridge had called Derrick. He'd known, all along. But by the look of shock on Derrick's face, he'd just found something he'd never known he had. Another brother.

And Charley envied him that unexpected gift.

****

They all ate hungrily, Billy and Rob both having their first taste of fry bread. Rob declared it one of the best foods God had ever created.

"God and the Cherokee," Carson corrected teasingly.

"I might have to take exception," Charley said with a laugh. "My mother made the best fry bread, bar none. But she was Seminole."

"Good food, no matter who started it," Spike said.

U. S. Deputy Marshal Atley Goodson, who was riding with the lighthorsemen, was someone that Derrick had taken an instant liking to. He was just an "honorary lighthorseman" this trip out, he told them, with a somber wink at Carson.

"What he's saying is," Carson explained with a grin, "he's riding along to be sure that when we catch up to the man we're after, we don't mete out justice if it's not warranted."

"Meaning?" Charley questioned.

"We're after a man who raped a Cherokee girl a week ago. We know who we're after."

"But, we don't know he's guilty, Ridge," Goodson said calmly, "or whose jurisdiction he's really under."

"He's Cherokee, Marshal."

Goodson chuckled. "Well, I'm sure when we catch up to him, one sight of you boys and he'll be shouting his white blood to Glory."

"He's Cherokee."

Goodson cocked his head. "I'm not sayin' he's not. Just not sayin' he is."

"Gotta be one or the other," the stone-faced officer spoke up.

"Not necessarily," Carson murmured quietly, his eyes on Derrick. "Not necessarily."

"What's the penalty for rape?" Spike asked.

"First offense, fifty lashes and losing the left ear. Second offense, a hundred lashes and losing the right ear," the short officer responded.

Spike gave a slow grin. "Well, I hate to ask, but bein' all out of ears, what if there's a third offense?"

"Then, he would lose his life," Carson said. "But in this case, the woman he raped has already forfeited hers. She drowned herself two days after he attacked her. So, this being his first offense, he'll come out ahead, it

175

seems, no matter what. Even with fifty lashes and no left ear, he will keep his life."

"If he's Cherokee," Goodson maintained doggedly.

"And if he's white?" Billy asked.

"Then he won't be losing body parts or skin," Goodson responded affably. "Only his freedom."

A few moments passed, and Billy, Spike and Rob rose one by one to turn in. Goodson and the quiet officer who had not spoken all evening left the clearing to keep watch until midnight when they would awaken the men who would relieve them.

Charley and the other two Cherokee officers played a game of dice, drinking a last cup of very strong coffee before turning in.

Derrick had been waiting for the chance to talk to Carson privately. He stood up and walked over to where his friend sat on a flat rock. So many years had passed. He and Carson had been friends, those first ten years of their lives, born within a week of one another. When Derrick's father had announced he was moving their family to Kansas, Derrick had thought he wouldn't be able to bear losing Carson.

But the days had slid into weeks, months rolled into years. His life in Indian Territory seemed far away, as they'd made a new life in Wolf Creek. And then, the War had come, robbing him of his father, his brothers and his self-worth, eventually.

Now...he stood over Carson, looking into his upturned face. To be reunited with a friend, and to gain a brother as well... He'd never even suspected, but the resemblance between the two of them was undeniable proof in itself.

If what Carson said was true, if they were brothers,

that meant…his father had never been his father. The man whose death he'd felt he had to avenge, had committed acts to do so that still kept him awake at night, had been no blood relation to him at all. The lifelong teasing from his older brothers had also been true. He had been 'different' and they'd never missed a chance to tell him so.

His mother…his thoughts turned to her, and Carson must have immediately seen it in his expression.

"Come sit. I'll tell you what I know."

"Lotta years—" Derrick sat on the ground beside Carson, just within the fire's far-reaching glow.

"I know, Derrick. But it doesn't change the past— what happened between our father, and our two mothers." He stopped and extended his arms, as if encompassing the world. "And the end result."

"Your father—"

"No. Our father." Carson's gaze bored into Derrick's. "He was in love with your mother, Derrick. He told me so. And she was in love with him. But they both had other…obligations. So, when it began to become obvious to others what had happened, your mother's husband seized the political issues in Kansas as a reason to move your family north."

Derrick was silent. He couldn't help but think of the way his father had treated him over the course of his lifetime. "Different." Even "cruel." His mother had intervened time and again until he'd asked her to stop. Now, it made sense. Now he understood everything.

And he was going to tell her so as soon as he got back to Wolf Creek.

"Convenient for him," Derrick said bitterly. "And if it hadn't been for us running into you here, I guess you and

I never would have been reunited. And I never would have known the truth." He fell silent a moment. "Moving to Kansas cost him his life. The Jayhawkers killed him."

"I'm sorry, Derrick. I thought you did know, by now—about us. I never thought your mother wouldn't tell you. I just believed you knew about me, but didn't want to acknowledge—" His voice trailed away.

"My Cherokee blood?" Thoughts of Charley's earlier remarks and his unreasoning anger at them washed over him.

Carson nodded. "That, and—your 'other brother.'"

"No." Derrick's voice was quiet. "I don't know why she didn't tell me. Especially now that—her husband is gone."

"She must've had her reasons."

"Where are you now?" Derrick asked, changing the subject.

"I moved up to Tahlequah last year." A smile crossed Carson's face. "Do you remember Jackson Ellis, our cousin?"

Derrick grinned. "Little 'tag along'?"

"He's Deputy Sheriff over Tahlequah District now."

"He's just a kid!"

"Twenty-two. He was appointed last year."

Derrick shook his head. The years had somehow come and gone more quickly than he'd realized. "I can't believe it. Seems like we all had to grow up fast, doesn't it?"

"Too fast. When will you be heading out?"

There was an urgency in Carson's tone that Derrick didn't mistake. He understood the question beneath the question.

"First light. But Carson, I'll be back. Soon as we

wrap this up tight, I'll be back. We've got lots of catching up to do."

Carson nodded. "Tahlequah. If I'm not there, find Jackson." His voice was low and warm. "You were not forgotten among our people, Derrick. There is still a place for you."

****

Just as the sky began to turn gray, Derrick strapped the last of his gear in place and said a final goodbye to his brother. He was surprised to see Marshal Goodson walking toward where the five Wolf Creek men had gathered.

"Mind if I ride along with y'all?"

Derrick had wondered how Goodson would handle the issue of a vigilante posse that had crossed into his jurisdiction. Now, he knew. He shot a quick look at Spike.

"Reckon we can always use an extra gun, Marshal," Charley said. "Be glad to have you."

Goodson nodded. "Figure we'll kill two birds with one stone. You'll get an extra gun and I'll keep y'all legal. I can see by the looks of you men you ain't goin' home 'til we see this done. This way, we can all have what we want. We'll get rid of this scum and do the world a favor. I don't want 'em in my territory any more than y'all want 'em back in Kansas."

"'Preciate your honesty, Marshal," Spike put in.

"And your gun," Billy added with a grin.

"Let's get after it, then." Derrick turned his horse southward, with a final goodbye salute to the Cherokee officers.

****

They reached the foothills of the San Bois Mountains by mid-afternoon that day. The terrain was rough and wild—and dry as Derrick could ever remember having seen it. But there was a heaviness to the air that more than hinted at the promise of rain.

They were closing the distance on Danby's men. Though Derrick knew where their Demon's Drop hideout was, they rode with caution. Charley had mentioned he didn't think Danby's outfit knew they were still being followed, and it made sense that they'd believe the Kansans would not have pursued them this deeply into Indian Territory. As arrogant as they were, at this point, and so close to safety, pursuit wouldn't be at the forefront of their minds. They were probably already figuring how they'd spend the money they'd stolen. But still, Derrick didn't want to take any chances.

Charley had told Derrick something else as they'd ridden side by side earlier that morning.

"When the shootin' starts, McCain, you can set your sights on any of 'em 'cept that tall, lanky redheaded bastard."

"Frank Davis?"

"Yep. I know him by name for a special reason. An' like I say, he's all mine."

Derrick had thrown him a sidelong glance. "Care to tell me why?"

"Be glad to. The son of a bitch killed my brother's son."

Though Charley's tone was as calm as if he were discussing the weather, Derrick understood that it was

Charley's way of being able to talk about something so deep.

"Cudjoe wasn't really my brother by blood, but we'd grown up together, and we was of a close age, though he was a bit older. Never let me forget it, either." His voice softened as he remembered. "Got into all kinds of scrapes, we did. Fought the U.S. Marines together in the Everglades. When my father was killed in what white folks called the Second Seminole War, Cudjoe took me in and watched over me." Charley gave a faint smile at the memories. "But after Osceola got taken and we got captured and ended up in these parts, him and my boys was killed in the fighting when we joined with Opothleyahola and broke for Kansas.

"I took his son, Sango, to live with me. We were with the Union forces at Centralia. That red headed bastard killed Sango. Cut off his head with a sword." Charley met Derrick's eyes, a questioning there that Derrick had to answer.

Derrick shook his head. "I know those things happened on both sides. But I didn't ever cut any man's head off, myself. Just like I never skinned any man alive." He gave a decisive nod "That wasn't my way. And you know that's true. I had held back at Centralia, I wasn't in the thick of it when you Yankees came charging in to the rescue, so I don't know what all happened there. But I'm sorry for your loss."

Charley seemed to be sizing him up again, trying to look into his mind. Finally, when Derrick thought the subject was closed, Charlie spoke again.

"It ain't just Sango's death I'm after him for. He was one of the ones shootin' at me and the other survivors, McCain. Just a little bit later, when your men—"

"Not my men," Derrick corrected hotly, tired of Charley's assumptions, sick of this talk of the War. "Remember, I got shot and was left for dead that day, same as you did."

Charley nodded, took a few seconds to form his answer.

"Yes. We was both left for dead that day, McCain. But Sango was mine to watch over and keep safe. I didn't do that. I failed, and he was cut down by Davis. He was young. Hadn't even seen sixteen summers yet. It was just a few minutes later when you and me met, if you can call it that. And just before we broke for it and they shot us, I recognized that bastard. I heard Danby call him Davis. I aim to kill him for what he did, and if I've got time, I plan to make it slow and hard on him."

It seemed to Derrick that Charley's dark face twisted briefly in emotion, although it may have been a trick of the light. "I couldn't avenge my sons. I never even seen them fall. But Sango, I seen who killed him. And I can be the blood avenger on that red-headed son of a bitch."

Derrick flexed his hand around the reins he held. "Well, fact is, I want him, too." He figured he might as well just let Charley know where he stood. "Davis was the one who shot me that day." His hand moved quickly across his chest, and Charley gave him a quick glance. "Today, I'll see him and raise. He's goin' home dead."

"Seems we both have old wounds to heal, and both need the same remedy. Which one of us will get it, I wonder?"

Derrick glanced back at the other four men. "Whichever one of us sees him first, I reckon. He'll be stiff before tomorrow, either way."

****

"Hey," Billy called.

"Fool kid," Charley growled, stopping to wait for Billy and the others to catch up to them.

Derrick grinned, drawing up, too.

"How much farther is this hideout?" Rob asked. "Got any idea?"

Spike looked around them, his head turning as he quartered their surroundings. The going had gotten rougher as the hilly trails became steeper, the horses' footing trickier.

Charley glanced at the sky. "Plenty of daylight left. And I'm betting we'll catch 'em in the next hour, maybe two."

Rob took a deep breath. "I'm ready to get this over with."

"So are we all," Spike said, resettling his kepi on his head.

Rob gave Spike a disgusted look, but didn't say anything more.

"We're not far off, now," Deputy Marshal Goodson said. "But we're not equipped to follow them much farther. Once they get holed up in these mountains—"

"Well, I ain't afraid of 'em," Rob said quickly. "Bunch of bastards. Ridin' in and doin' what they did—"

"You'd better be afraid, son," the marshal responded. "If they've done what you say, and if they're part of Danby's riders, they're a force to be reckoned with. I hope you live through this. You're young. Maybe, comin' out on the other side of what we're facing will allow you some—understanding."

Billy and Rob had both been too young to march off

to war, Derrick thought. Neither of them were afraid...yet. But the fact was, there was only one way up this mountain that wouldn't take more time than they had before Danby's men got too far ahead of them to catch. He saw the look that passed between Spike and the marshal. They'd be damn lucky to ride back to Kansas, all of them, without leaving any of their group dead. He turned his horse back toward the trail, and they started off again in the stifling heat.

CHAPTER TWELVE

The first bullet whined past Derrick's head, catching Rob low in the right side. The impact knocked him from the saddle. The sudden, ferocious pain as the lead tracked through his flesh, into his body, surprised him, and he yelled as he fell. The breath rushed out of him as he hit the ground.

"Take cover!" Goodson called out, but his order was unnecessary. The others were off their horses, scrambling for the brush as bullets sang around them, kicking up dust and chipping rock.

As Derrick hit the ground he pulled his rifle from his saddle scabbard, snagging his canteen in the same motion. In spite of their circumstances, he had to smile, and in the next instant utter a curse. By the weight of it, it was half-empty—again.

He looked around from where he'd taken cover behind a raised outcropping of rock. He couldn't see any of the others except Charley, who'd been riding close to him when the lead had begun to fly. He crouched to Derrick's left.

Charley was looking at something over Derrick's head, and when Derrick looked up the trail on the left side, he saw the top of a light-colored straw hat.

Charley raised the scarred Yellowboy carefully, sighting down the barrel and squeezed the trigger. The hat disappeared, and a sharp cry of pain came from the same area where the man had been.

A frenzied volley of bullets erupted from the outlaws' guns. Derrick waited, careful about his shots. In the shimmering heat of the rocks and crevasses of these mountains, it was difficult to see. He only hoped the Wolf Creek posse was hidden from sight as well as Danby's men were. He reached up to wipe the sweat out of his eyes. In the distance, he could hear Rob whimper. Derrick knew that sound well. When he glanced at Charley, the black man shook his head.

"I hoped to God I wouldn't be hearin' that today," Charley muttered.

"Who's with him? Can you see?"

"Looked to me like Sweeney was helpin' him, last I saw. They was riding close."

"Goodson? Marshal Goodson! Is that you?" a voice called from near the brush where Charley had shot earlier. It wasn't the man he'd hit, Derrick felt certain. The way he'd cried out was also a familiar sound—the sound of a man being mortally wounded, and realizing it the moment before he died.

"You bet your sweet runnin' scared ass it's me!" Goodson replied from a few feet behind where Charley and Derrick squatted. "Who'm I talkin' to?"

"Reckon I'm the leader of this outfit, Marshal. Jim Danby."

"Well, Danby, I've brought some help with me, and we're prepared to take you in—see that y'all get a fair trial."

Danby laughed. "How 'bout we ride on our separate ways? You all mosey on back north, and we'll go on up into these here mountains. We'll maybe tangle another time. Right now, we've got us some money to divvy up and figure out how to spend. And we want to thank all the good people of Wolf Creek kindly for that."

"Don't be so hasty, Danby. Some of those 'good people' have ridden a long way to see you brought to justice—one way or the other. How many men do you have?"

"Enough," came the curt reply. "An' I do believe I seen one of my men in your midst earlier. How you doin' Derrick? Last I saw of your sorry ass, you was bleedin' like you was gonna die."

"Yeah, but I didn't, Jim," Derrick answered.

"My mistake. I should of done it myself instead of givin' it to Davis to do. Maybe we can fix that today."

"I don't plan on that, Danby," Derrick responded. He glanced at Charley. "I wish to hell we could get around back of them," he told the scout.

"I don't see how," Charley said softly. "They know where we are, even how many of us there are—"

"Once it gets dark, it's all over."

Charley nodded.

They were truly at a standoff. For the Wolf Creek men to make a move directly up the trail would be suicide. Going around from this point, would be impossible due to the lack of cover. Danby's men held the advantage of having the higher ground.

Just then, the sound of a scuffle behind an outcropping of shale sounded at about the point where Danby's voice had come from. Charley and Derrick looked at one another.

"What the hell?" Derrick muttered.

In the next instant, a shot rang out and Danby gave a startled yelp, then fell out into the open from behind the scrub brush where he'd been concealed. His body rolled a few feet and then came to a stop, sightless eyes staring heavenward, a fountain of red bubbling out from his chambray shirt to stain the rocky ground beneath him.

"That's for Wolf Creek, you son of a bitch!"

"Satterlee," Derrick breathed.

Charley's smile was wide. "Well, let's give him some help!"

Satterlee's repeater was already blazing from his vantage point, forcing some of Danby's men to have to choose death at his hands or scramble for better cover, coming out into the open as they ran.

Goodson's Henry and Sweeney's Austrian joined the blasts of Derrick and Charley's to lay down a deadly barrage of bullets.

Suddenly, one of the outlaws stood up from where he'd been hiding—no more than thirty feet from where Sweeney and Gallagher had taken cover.

Blood covered his chest and trickled from his mouth. He pitched forward onto the ground, a surprised look on his face. His hat fell beside him, revealing a head of red hair. Derrick and Charley were both instantly on their feet, running toward him. They pulled him back into the shelter of the bush, where only Sheriff Satterlee was behind them.

"You bastard!" Charley exploded. He quickly drew his long blade from its sheath, and Davis's eyes widened in fear. "I've got you. An' I been waitin' on this day a long, long time. Remember Centralia? You cut down a black boy—though I'm sure you never gave it another thought. Last I saw of you, you was ridin' off, laughin' and wipin' that Reb sword of yours clean of his blood."

Charley put his knife close to the man's head,

grabbing a handful of his hair, his intention clear.

"No!" Davis yelled. "I'm dyin'!"

"Yeah. You sure as hell are. This is for every murder you ever did in this life, Davis, but mostly for Sango Chedakis at Centralia."

"I never did that…I wasn't…there…"

"Yes, you did. I saw you. Now," Charley looked at his blade, then held it up to gleam in the sun, "it's your turn. 'Course, it won't be as clean as what you did—with a sword. And it'll take a mite longer." He bared his teeth at Davis. "You'll have a while to feel it, Davis. Every second of it."

"That—that wasn't me!" Davis spat blood, then swallowed. "Clark?" he called.

If the shooting hadn't all but stopped, the others couldn't have heard the thin, reedy voice.

"Clark! Run! Get out of here—"

Derrick looked at Charley, then back at Frank Davis.

"You, I done, McCain. Blasted you to…to hell…and here you are—still alive." Davis' mouth twisted in pain, but Derrick couldn't miss the smirk as well. His jaw tensed at that. Seemed Charley and he neither one was going to get the full satisfaction of what they wanted to do to Davis. He was nearly gone.

Davis'eyes sought Charley's "What you said…I didn't…never carried no sword…"

"Then who? Who?" Charley shook him, hard, but Davis smiled as he took his last breath, safe in the knowledge that his secret was still untold.

"It was him," Charley muttered, sitting back on his heels. "I don't care what he said—"

"No," Derrick said quietly. "No." He began to rifle the dead man's pockets. There may be something, he thought. Davis wouldn't have lied about Sango Chedakis, he didn't think—there was something in the dying man's face that made Derrick believe him. 'Clark,' Davis had called. A warning. His fingers closed around something hard, and he drew it from Davis' pocket.

A tintype. He turned it over. Two boys stared out at him. Both had light hair and freckles. Both were thin-faced and of nearly the same height. Derrick turned the picture over. Cousins Clark and Frank Davis, someone had penciled on the metal. And beneath that, 1855.

Derrick swore harshly. "Clark." His voice was filled with self-reproach. He handed the picture to Charley. "Of course. I didn't think about that. His cousin, Clark—he rode with us, and he was there that day. I don't think he had been with us for long, so I plumb forgot about him. And now I think on it, I remember—Frank never did carry a saber, he always used a big Bowie knife. Same one that's on his belt now, I reckon. They resemble each other enough—it wasn't Frank, Charley. It had to be his cousin that killed your friend's boy. You didn't see them both together, and it all happened mighty fast."

"Damn it!"

The other Wolf Creek men were coming out to meet Sheriff Satterlee as he made his way down the mountainside, stopping now and again to make sure each one of Danby's men that had been shot was dead. He took a minute when he reached Danby's body to kick him in the ribs. There was no response. A grin spread across his weathered face. "Burn in hell you son of a bitch," he said savagely.

"Amen to that!" Goodson agreed from a few yards away.

Charley rose swiftly, scanning the woods around

them, but there was no sign of any live captives. "Maybe Satterlee got him," he muttered, starting toward the sheriff. A low groan of pain escaped him as he took a step, the second step slower than the first.

Derrick stood up and followed him, the two of them reaching a break in the cover of the thick brush and trees just in time to see a flash of brightly-colored red shirt tail flapping in the breeze atop a gray mount. The blur of color disappeared over a distant ridge. Charley let go a curse and stumbled forward, but Derrick caught him and held on. "Let him go, Charley."

"What the hell?"

"Look at you! You're shot."

Charley looked down as if just realizing he'd been wounded. Blood flowed freely from a tear in his pants, two inches above his right kneecap. "Damn it! He's getting away!"

Derrick shook his head. "He's gone, Charley. And none of us is in much shape to go after him—especially not so close to Demon's Drop as we are."

He'd gotten the salve for his own open wound of vengeance he'd carried so long, Derrick thought. Jim Danby was dead, just as he'd vowed he would be, and Frank Davis too. But Charley Blackfeather's healing would have to wait.

****

Spike Sweeney propped Rob Gallagher up under the meager shade of a scrubby brush, resting his head on a stone. The young man whimpered when the blacksmith jostled him.

A forced smile appeared on Rob's wan face. "I

reckon I'm done for," he said weakly. "I never expected to make it this far, to tell the truth."

Sweeney ripped his own bandanna in half and shoved one part of it into Rob's wound as makeshift packing. "Talk like that don't do anybody no good," Spike said gruffly. Then, in a gentler tone, he added, "You'll be back at that general store slingin' flour sacks around in no time."

Spike wet the other half of the bandanna sparingly with water from his own canteen and used it to dab the sweat from Rob's pale face.

"I'm ashamed, Spike," the younger man said.

"Ain't nothin' to be ashamed of, son," the blacksmith said. "You've done good. We'll make sure everybody back in town knows what a hellcat you've been, and when they see you in the street they'll tip their hat and call you sir. Gettin' shot like this, it's just bad luck. No shame at all."

"I don't mean that," Rob said. "I'm ashamed of the way I treated you, and the things I said."

"It was just words, son."

Rob closed his eyes as a wave of pain washed over him. When he opened them again they were tinged with agonized tears. Spike took off his gray kepi and placed it on Rob's head—he had lost his hat—to shade his eyes from the sun.

"My pa was an abolitionist," Rob said weakly. "He brought us down here from Ohio when I was a little kid. Him and my uncles fought with John Brown at Osawatomie. When I was eleven some Rebs shot him down in the field where we was workin'."

"A lot of bad things happened back then," Spike said, "on both sides. I understand how somethin' like that can color your outlook."

"I think that's why I fought so hard, so much harder than I knew I could, back yonder at the ambush. Those outlaws was the same kind of people that killed my pa—and so was you. At least that's what I thought. But you ain't like them, I was wrong."

"You hush now, Mister Gallagher," Spike said kindly. "Save your breath, and don't worry none about them things. Bygones is gone by, my father used to say. You just rest."

Rob closed his eyes, and soon was unconscious. Spike feared he was dead at first. Then the blacksmith realized someone was standing over him—it was Derrick McCain.

"How is he?" Derrick asked.

"Not good," Spike answered shortly. He drew a deep breath and let it out in a long sigh. "Not much I could do for him under the circumstances. We need to round up our animals and hightail it back to the nearest doc."

"That would be in Tahlequah—a good two-day ride from here."

"He won't make it," Spike said.

"No."

Just then, Sheriff Satterlee and Billy made their way over.

"Sheriff." Spike nodded at Satterlee. "It sure as hell is good to see you."

Satterlee grinned. "You boys got yourselves into a jam. Wouldn't be right for me not to come help you out of it."

"What happened?" Billy asked. "We thought you were back in Wolf Creek."

Satterlee squatted beside Rob, giving a cursory glance

to the temporary bandage. He shook his head. "I got to thinkin' 'bout ridin' back to Wolf Creek. I'm a law man. Here y'all were, trackin' down these sonsabitches, and me goin' home. Couldn't do it. I had to turn around and come back to help. Been trailin' you now for days, but I just couldn't push my horse any harder in this heat."

"It all worked out," Marshal Goodson put in as he approached the others. "I kept an eye on this bunch until you came back to claim 'em" He stuck his hand out. "U.S. Deputy Marshal Atley Goodson."

"Sheriff George Washington Satterlee. Much obliged." Satterlee's expression became serious again as he looked down at Rob. "We need to figure out what's best for him. Where's the nearest town?"

"Tahlequah," Derrick answered. "Too far."

"There's a place a few miles east of here," Goodson said thoughtfully. "Tamaha. Not big, but close. And there may be someone there he can stay with 'til he's well enough to ride. They're good people over there."

"I'll stay with him," Billy volunteered.

"No," Spike said. "I'll stay."

Derrick and Satterlee exchanged a questioning glance.

"You, Spike?" Satterlee asked incredulously. "Thought there wasn't any love lost between you two. It's no secret y'all fought on opposite sides—"

Spike gave a faint smile. "Rob never fought in no War, G. W. He was just a boy. Too young. I reckon all of us can stand to learn a thing or two. I understand some things about Mister Gallagher I didn't know before."

"Such as?" Billy asked.

But Spike shook his head. "He'll tell you someday, maybe. I will say this—anybody who's seen his father killed in cold blood by vigilantes from the 'other side' has a right to hate. And sometimes, it takes a long, long time to see that all men aren't alike. There's good and bad on both sides, gray and blue." He looked around the group. "And I know there's more'n one of us that's thought like that, had the same type of thing happen in their own families. I just hope some day we can get over all that's happened in the past during that godawful war, and afterward." He paused. "Today is my day, I guess." He looked down at Rob, a wry smile touching his lips. "He'll never believe he wore my cap."

Satterlee snorted. "He'll never believe you're the one who saved him."

Spike nodded and met Satterlee's amused expression. "He'll believe, all right. Once I get a chance to talk to him."

Charley limped toward them, leading his and Derrick's mounts. "You comin' with me?"

"Now, hold up a minute, Charley," Spike said. "Looks like you're wantin' to go on after the one that got away. We've gotta get Gallagher, here, to a doc. That's gotta be the priority—not chasin' that damn owlhoot farther up into the mountains." He glanced past Charley toward the steep, rocky trail that let into dense cover.

"Not askin' you to string along with me, Sweeney," Charley replied curtly. "You want to see to Gallagher, go on." He glanced at Derrick again. "Comin', McCain?"

Before Derrick could reply, Sheriff Satterlee said, "No, he ain't. An' neither are you. We're gonna get this wounded man to help, before Danby's man that escaped can get back to their hideout and bring hell down on us. For all we know they've got more men waiting there."

"'Fraid I have to agree, Blackfeather," Goodson

spoke up. "I'm going to have to accompany y'all over to Tamaha to get this man some medical help." He nodded at Charley's bloody leg. "Looks like you could use tendin' yourself."

"All I need, Marshal, is a hank of red hair on my coup stick. That'd be the best medicine I could get. You don't need all of us to go see that Gallagher gets treated. I'm after Davis."

Sheriff Satterlee's expression had softened. "I gather you know that bastard and have some history with him. I can sympathize with that. The fact is, though, Jim Danby hit our town with a small army—and we've sent almost the whole bunch to hell where they belong. That's a pretty good job of work. It's a shame that one got away, but there'll be other days."

Goodson gave the Seminole a slow smile. "Don't put me agin' you, Blackfeather. I'm on your side. But I've never figured out how to be two places at once. I can't ride with you and McCain and show these men where to take Gallagher, here. And right now, Gallagher needs me more than you need your all-fired vengeance."

"I don't need you, Marshal Goodson," Charley replied evenly.

"Yes, you do. I won't tolerate vigilantes down here in my territory. It's lawless enough as it is, with less than two hundred of us marshals at any given time to see to it. And right now, like I say, I can't be in two places at once. Once we get Gallagher seen to, I'll be glad for your help—as a deputized member of a legal posse. That might be a few days. Now, if you'll excuse me, I need to go make a record of these dead men's names, best I can figure, and see about rounding up the other horses." Goodson turned away, the subject closed.

Charley's face was impassive, but his eyes glittered with anger and determination.

"Charley, he's right," Derrick said with a sigh. He reached for the reins that Charley held in his left hand. "We're tired, the horses are exhausted and Gallagher's gotta have a doc or he's not gonna make it. You need one, yourself. Look at you—you're barely standin' on that leg."

"Well, you sure changed your tune, McCain. Ready to quit and go home. But there's still one of 'em out there. The one I want. And I ain't ridin' over to Tamaha to get this lead dug out. I'll do it my own self."

Derrick shook his head. "Damn stubborn mule. There'll be another time. I'll come back with you."

Charley gave a short, mirthless laugh. "Thanks. For nothin'. By now, he's gone, for sure. Probably sittin' up there with a bunch of other bastards at Demon's Drop where he knows damn well we can't get to him."

Derrick remained silent for a long moment, his gaze holding Charley's. "That's right, Charley. He may already be there, or near enough to where we'd do nothin' but get our own selves killed by whoever else is up there. You're in no shape to go after anyone right now. I'm not ready to die today. Are you?"

He put his hand on Charley's shoulder as the Seminole started to turn away, then slipped his shoulder under Charley's arm as he faltered from the weakened leg. "Charley—remember that night when we talked. You said you were gonna be watching me. You talked about balance. Well, that's what I'm askin' you for right now. Balance. We got to weigh the good against the bad. The right of goin' on after this other Davis against the wrong of not seein' to our own wounded, our own horseflesh—

our own selves."

Charley watched Derrick now, listening, but still ready to turn away at a moment's notice, though he leaned heavily on Derrick now.

Derrick continued quickly. Charley's weight let Derrick know his ability to stand was waning, fast. "We can't let Gallagher die out here so you and I can go off after vengeance for something that happened six years ago. This is what I learned from the War, Charley. The minute I turned against Danby and defended you, refused to do his bidding, I became a man again. Just a man. No blue or gray. No black, or white, or even red. So, I'm asking you today, to come back to Wolf Creek with the rest of us. Let's see to our own. Let's patch up their wounds and the rips in our own hearts and souls that never seem to quit trickling our life's blood, no matter how many years pass. Don't let that damned war steal the rest of your life, Charley."

"I'll never put it behind me until I see that bastard dead. I have to see it done before I die, McCain."

Derrick put up a hand. "All right. Come home and heal a little first. We're all only men. We all have a breaking point." He hesitated. "I promise you, in a few weeks, we'll head back this way, and I'll help you track Clark Davis down." He reached to pull his bandanna from his pocket, motioning Charley to the ground. "Let's at least tie up your leg and get the bleedin' stopped."

"The trail will be cold," Charley said doggedly, lowering himself to sit on the parched earth. But he stretched his leg out with a grimace, and Derrick encircled it with his bandanna. "We're so close now!"

"Derrick's right, Charley," Satterlee spoke up. "We don't want to lose any more good men going after one bad one. We're out of our jurisdiction now, anyhow."

Charley snorted. "I don't give a damn about jurisdiction. He killed Sango! That boy was under my protection. Don't you understand?"

"Reckon I do," Satterlee said. "But I know this, too. We've all lost a brother, father—someone in this War and what came after in these years past. I know your two boys were killed. And I know this Sango was like kin to you. We do understand—all of us. You ain't the only one, you know. Hell, we have four good men in shallow graves back yonder, not to mention Haskins and his wife, that are still waitin' on a proper burial, one of 'em my best friend." Satterlee turned away to leave Derrick to finish tying up Charley's wound. The sheriff shook his head as he walked toward where Goodson and Billy were hoisting Rob Gallagher up into the saddle in front of Spike Sweeney on Sweeney's horse, hurrying to put a supporting hand to Rob's side.

Charley's gaze followed the sheriff to where they worked to get the wounded man in position. "Guess we can't leave him to bleed to death," he muttered.

"Or you, either, you damn stubborn Indian." Derrick muttered as he stood up.

"There's been enough blood on this trail we've followed to last me a lifetime," Charley said roughly, "...after I see Clark Davis dead."

"I'll help you, Charley. That's a promise."

Charley threw him a sidelong look as Derrick put a hand out to pull him up. "Seems you found something on this journey you didn't know you had."

"What's that?" Derrick stood close by as Charley tested his leg to see if it would bear his weight.

"A brother, Cherokee."

Derrick laughed. "Not just Carson, Charley. After what you and I have been through, I consider you a brother of sorts, too."

Charley turned away to hide his smile. "You and me? A Seminole and a Cherokee?"

Derrick glanced up the mountainside toward where Marshal Goodson stood. "Now you're talkin'. You didn't mention my white half or your black half, my gray or your blue."

After a minute, Charley said, "They say we both come from one of the five 'Civilized Tribes.'"

Thunder rolled in the near distance, the summer storm that Charley had predicted on the way. The wind had picked up.

Derrick looked around the group. Spike Sweeney, carefully holding Rob Gallagher's body against him as they waited for the others to mount up. Rob, the first one hit in the firefight in spite of his arsenal of weaponry and his diligent practice. Young Billy Below, who stood, expertly securing the string of horses—including the one carrying the money from the Wolf Creek Savings & Loan—in preparation for the long ride back. Sheriff G.W. Satterlee, who had tossed the rules of the law he loved so much to the wind and soothed his conscience by returning to help them, maybe making the difference between their success or their deaths. Deputy Marshal Goodson, who had thrown in with them in his own need to keep things legal and had lent his support to their cause. And Charley Blackfeather, whose friendship had, as far as Derrick was concerned, turned out to be almost the biggest surprise of all—aside from learning the truth about his own family. They'd done what they set out to do—fought back for their town and shown Danby and others like him that Wolf Creek took care of its own. They'd recovered the money in the process; though that had not been the reason they'd come together as they had, men of all blood, who just a few years ago would have killed each other for wearing gray or blue. They'd lost much, Derrick thought, the citizens of Wolf Creek. But look at what we've gained. And now, it was over—but life would never be the same in their town.

Derrick drew a deep breath. "Yeah, Charley, but right now, we're all just men. Tired and ready to go back to where we belong. Back to find our balance, as you say."

"Wolf Creek." Charley said, in simple agreement.

The rain began to fall as they mounted up. The cleansing drizzle covered them. It was the answer to an unspoken prayer for forgiveness, with a promise of peace for them all. The posse made their way back down through the winding path of the foothills. When they reached the open country below, three veered eastward, to Tamaha. The other four headed north, toward Kansas. The rain settled into a steady shower of heaven-sent hope. It washed away the bloody trail of vengeance, the rhythm of it singing in their veins.

Home… Home.

THE END

ABOUT THE AUTHORS:

JAMES J. GRIFFIN

I've been in love with horses and fascinated by all things Western, in particular the Texas Rangers, since I was a kid, so when I started writing it was only natural I would write Texas Ranger novels. Luckily, I have my good friends, Texas Ranger Jim Huggins of Company A, and Karl Rehn and Penny Riggs of KR Training in Manheim, Texas, to help with my research. Jim provides advice on the Rangers, while Karl and Penny lend their expertise on weapons of the period. I also travel out West every chance I get for research and relaxation. My two main series are about Texas Rangers Jim Blawcyzk and Cody Havlicek. The books are all very traditional Westerns, and most are suitable for almost all ages.   As a lifelong horseman, there's nothing I like better than climbing into the saddle and getting out into the hills and woods for the day, just me and my horse. While I love everything about the West, I love my native New England, particularly my adopted home state of New Hampshire, even more, and live for the day, not far off now, when I'll be able to move back up North for good. Right now I split my time between Branford, Connecticut, where I work, and Keene, New Hampshire. Two best friends are my horse, Yankee, and my Shih Tzu, Dogie.

My website is www.jamesjgriffin.net.

L. J. MARTIN

I am the author of 25 western, historical, mystery, and

thriller novels from Bantam, Pinnacle, Avon, and Wolfpack Publishing, and of five non-fiction works. I live in Montana with my wife, Kat, the New York Times bestselling author of over 55 romantic suspense and historical romance novels internationally published in a dozen languages and more than two dozen countries. When not writing, I spend a good deal of my time running a conservative political blog at http://fromthepeapatch.com, working with my horses, hunting, fishing, cooking, and wandering the back country with my cameras, both video and still. My photography has appeared on national magazine covers and in periodicals. Over one hundred of my videos can be seen on youtube.com at ljmartinwolfpack. Learn more about the Martins at www.ljmartin.com and www.katmartin.com.

CLAY MORE
My real name is Keith Souter and I was born in St Andrews in Scotland. I studied Medicine at Dundee University and then practiced as a family doctor in the city of Wakefield in England for thirty years. While I was at medical school I started to write children's stories for a family magazine, but after qualifying as a doctor the exigencies of the job were such that the focus of my writing was on medicine. I have also been a health columnist for almost thirty years and have written about a dozen medical and health books. In addition I write non-fiction books including *Schoolboy Science Remembered; The Pocket Guide to Dice and Dice Games; The Little Book of Genius; The Little Book of Golf; Medical Meddlers, Mediums and Magicians – the Victorian Age of Credulity* and *The Classic Guide to King Arthur.* Using

the pen-name of Clay More I write traditional westerns with the Black Horse Westerns imprint of Hale of London: *Raw Deal at Pasco Springs; Nemesis for the Judge; Double-Dealing at Dirtville; A Rope for Scudder* and *Stampede at Rattlesnake Pass.* I also write Scottish-based crime novels as Keith Moray for Hale: *The Gathering Murders; Deathly Wind; Murder Solstice* and *Flotsam and Jestsam.* In 2006 I won a Fish Prize for my short historical story *A Villain's Tale* and writing as Keith Souter started a series of historical mysteries set around Sandal Castle, the ruined medieval castle that I live within arrowshot of: *The Pardoner's Crime* and *The Fool's Folly.* In the summer of 2012 the first in my series of Victorian children's adventures begins with *The Curse of the Body Snatchers* by G-Press. My website is www.keithsouter.co.uk and my blog is http://west-uist-chronicle.blogspot.co.uk
[I am a member of the Society of Authors, The Crime Writers' Association, Medical Journalists' Association, International Thriller Writers, Western Writers of America and Western Fictioneers.]

CHERYL PIERSON
A native Oklahoman, I was born in Duncan, OK, and grew up in Seminole, OK. I graduated from the University of Oklahoma, and hold a B.A. in English. I've taught numerous writing classes and workshops over the past years throughout the OKC metro area. I live with my husband in Oklahoma City, OK, where we've been for the past 28 years. I have two grown children, ages 22 and 25. My short story, "The Kindness of Strangers," is included in the Western Fictioneers anthology *The Traditional West.* Other western short stories you might

be interested in are: "Homecoming," "Scarlet Ribbons," "Every Girl's Dream," "One Magic Night," "Meant to Be" and "Jason's Angel," all available through Western Trail Blazer (WTB) publishing. My novella, *Kane's Redemption*, the first of a series, is also available through WTB, as well as my time travel western novel, *Time Plains Drifter*. Also, look for my upcoming releases, *Fire Eyes*, a western novel, and *Kane's Promise*, the second novella in the "Kane" series, through WTB. Also, be on the lookout for my holiday short story, "The Keepers of Camelot," that will be included in the Western Fictioneers anthology, *Six Guns and Slay Bells: A Creepy Cowboy Christmas*. You can visit my website at http://www.cherylpierson.com. You can e-mail me at fabkat_edit@yahoo.com (I love to hear from readers and other authors!) *All books and short stories available at:* *https://www.amazon.com/author/cherylpierson*

JAMES REASONER

I write novels and short stories for a living (although I'll occasionally write a short story for a non-paying market if it's something I really want to do) and book and movie reviews for fun on my blog, which can be found at http://jamesreasoner.blogspot.com. I started out as a mystery writer nearly 35 years ago and still work in that genre and others, but I've done more Westerns than anything else. I've been married to best-selling, award-winning author, uncredited collaborator, editor, and plotter Livia J. Washburn for nearly 35 years. (Note the similarity between the length of my marriage and the length of my writing career. Coincidence? I don't think so.) We live in the same small town in Texas where we both grew up, although it's not so small anymore. (We have a Wal-Mart now!) After all these years, I still love to write and can't imagine doing anything else. My website is www.jamesreasoner.net.

TROY D. SMITH

I am from the Upper Cumberland region of Tennessee. My work has appeared in many anthologies, and in journals such as *Louis L'Amour Western Magazine, Civil War Times,* and *Wild West.* In addition, I've written novels in several genres—from mysteries like *Cross Road Blues* to the Civil War epic *Good Rebel Soil.* My other Civil War epic, *Bound for the Promise-Land,* won a Spur Award in 2001 and I was a finalist on two other occasions. Two of my short stories are finalists for this year's Peacemaker Award for western fiction. In a massive lapse of collective judgment, the membership of Western Fictioneers elected me president for 2012. I received my Ph.D. from the University of Illinois, and teach American Indian history at Tennessee Tech. My motto is: "I don't write about things that happen to people, I write about people that things happen to." My website is www.troyduanesmith.com , and my blog is http://tnwordsmith.blogspot.com .

<u>The Wolf Creek series:</u>
Book 1: Bloody Trail
Book 2: Kiowa Vengeance
Book 3: Dogleg City
Book 4: The Taylor County War

More to come!

Coming soon:

October 2012

Also available from Western Fictioneers:

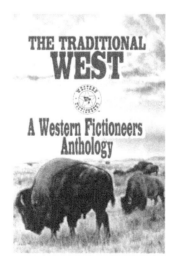

Western Fictioneers

Made in the USA
Coppell, TX
26 February 2023

13451045R10118